D1520656

Torn between Love and Lust

By

Chantel

"Torn Between Love and Lust"

Copyright © 2019 by Chantel

Published by Tyanna Presents

All rights reserved.

☐

Synopsis

When you start questioning your love for your spouse, then it really isn't love. Lust can land you in an unpredictable situation.

Meet Kadeem Holly; twenty-eight and a very independent woman. Even though she's supposed to be happily married, she still feels that something is missing. She busted her tail to make sure her husband, Tyrese, was straight, when it should have been the other way around.

Ahkeem Fisher is a thirty-one-year-old millionaire. He wasn't a dope boy, nor had he ever been in the streets. He worked the hard and legit way to get where he is today, but being on top doesn't allow room for a real relationship, nor did he want one, until he fell for a married woman.

Meeting Kadeem wasn't a coincident; they hit it off because they wanted the same things in life. What was said to be lust quickly turned into love. Will Kadeem remember that she is a married woman and end the fling that began in desire, or will Ahkeem have her doing things that she has never done before but always wanted to do?

Sit back and enjoy the ride in Torn between Love and Lust!

Table of Contents:

Prologue

Angelica

"Ty, when you gon' stop playin' and come be with your family? I know you got a wife, but you also have a daughter that needs your ass," Angelica fussed. She was making my damn head hurt with all the nagging. I wish she would shut the fuck up!

"When the time is right, I will be with y'all. Stop bumping your gums and come suck this dick," I told her, jerking my dick up and down. I saw the lust in her eyes, and I knew she couldn't resist a nigga. Shit, if I were me, I wouldn't be able to resist me either. I was a fly nigga if I must say so myself.

She crawled over to me and eased my dick in her mouth. After adjusting to my size, she went to town on my dick. Starting slow, she started picking up speed, had my damn eyes rolling in the back of my head. Angelica could be the perfect woman if she didn't nag so damn much. Her ass was worse than Kadeem, Kadeem knew her place and stayed in it.

"Fuck girl, you better suck that dick and stop playing with him," I told her, and she started sucking the skin off my dick. She was letting the spit fall out of her mouth, just like I liked it. I was a nasty nigga that liked nasty shit.

"Damn Ty, your dick taste so fuckin' good," she moaned, sending an electric shock through my shit.

I won't lie, Angelica's head game was the truth, Kadeem didn't have shit on her. Angelica had a nigga's toes throwing up all kinda gang signs. After fucking her face a little more, I sent my nut deep down her throat. Like the nasty bitch she was, she swallowed without hesitation.

"You ready for this dick?" I asked her, getting my dick back up. My shit was like the energizer bunny, he kept going and going.

Angelica laid on her back and spread her legs wide open, giving me easy access to the pussy. I wasted no time sliding inside her ocean. No lie, pussy so good had a nigga thinkin' about proposing to her ass. I'm just fucking with y'all, but y'all get the picture.

"Fuck girl, why your shit gotta be so good?" I asked her, backing out the pussy. Pussy was about to have a nigga bustin', and I was just getting started.

"Ty, I'm about to cum!" she screamed as her eyes rolled in the back of her head. Just where I wanted them bitches to be in the back of her damn head.

Shortly after, I was cumming deep inside her. I knew this was so wrong, but it felt so right. Rolling off her, I looked down at my dick and realized I wasn't wearing a condom. My ass had been fucking up lately, and if Kadeem ever found out, she would leave a nigga no questions asked. Closing my eyes for a quick minute, my ass was out for the count. I had turned my phone off earlier, so I didn't have a care in the world. I knew Kadeem was gonna be pissed, but once I gave her some of this dick, she would forget about being mad.

While I was sleep, I slowly felt my dick rising, and I knew Angelica was teasing him. She knew how to make my dick hard without even trying to, but I wasn't mad at baby girl, I just let her do her thang.

"Damn Kadeem, your mouth wet as hell," I slipped up and said. My eyes popped open realizing that I had just called her Kadeem. I just prayed that she didn't hear that shit.

"Nigga, you tried it calling me that bitch name. I put up with a lot of shit, but I won't put up with the disrespect," she spat, popping my dick out her mouth. Damn, I didn't mean to call her Kadeem, I knew that I was fucking up.

"My bad, Angelica, it's not even like that. My ass was caught up in the moment, and that shit slipped," I informed her as she started throwing shit. "I said I was sorry, damn. What I'm not gon' do is kiss yo' ass. I said I was working through some shit, and we will be together in due time. Take that shit or not, but there ain't no way out of this. There is no fucking way you gon' take my daughter from me. Now take that shit how you want. Come on so I can give your ass some more of this act right," I told her, meaning everything I had said.

She wasn't into it no more, but I didn't give a damn as long as I got my nut. Fuck her feelings. It was crazy because I loved her and Kadeem, just in different ways. Ain't that about a bitch!

***

Kadeem

"Shay, I swear to God, Tyrese ass better not be in this bitch. After all this shit, and he wanna play me, I believe the fuck not," I damn near yelled. Shay's ass was sitting in the passenger seat a little too calm for me. I was trying to be calm, but I wanted to fuck some shit up right now.

"Kadeem, I think you're blowing this all out of proportion. There is no way in hell that Tyrese is in there. This man loves you and your dirty drawls," she mentioned to me, and I wasn't convinced. We were sitting outside the Hampton Inn. Tyrese thought he could get over on me, but I had tracked his phone. Call me what you want, but you can't call me a dumb bitch.

Tyrese had done some fucked up shit, but he had never openly cheated. He might have lied to me, but I had never witnessed him cheating. If I caught him in the act, I don't know if I could stay with him. My pride wasn't gonna let me.

Slowly exiting the car, Shay and I made our way inside the hotel. We were greeted by a very chipper receptionist. She was looking too happy for me. I just hoped that my plan pulled through.

"Welcome to Hampton Inn, my name is Shatavia. Double bed or king?" she asked us, and I looked at Shay. She was looking at me like I was crazy, but I needed her back with this one. I couldn't blow this, I needed to catch him in the act.

"Good evening, I'm here to set up before my husband arrives. He told me that I could come get the key from you," I lied. The bitch just stared at me like she was reading my mind or some shit. *Damn, I hope this bitch couldn't see how nervous I was.*

"I'm sorry, ma'am, what's your husband's name, and I can look it up for you. I would have to call him to confirm though," she told me.

"Don't do that, I want this to be a surprise. Today is our fifteenth wedding anniversary," I told her, hoping she would take the bait.

"What's your husband's name? I can see about making an exception for you. I hope that one day I find a man and stay married as long as y'all," she told me, and she had to be the dumbest bitch for taking the bait.

"Tyrese Holly," I told her, and she started typing away on her computer.

"Here you go, ma'am, it's room number 417. Happy anniversary, and enjoy your stay," she told me as I grabbed the room key.

"Bitch, you did it. She didn't ask your ass for shit, and her ass could really lose her job for this," Shay told me, and I shrugged. I got what I wanted, I didn't give a damn about her being jobless. Call me selfish if you want to.

We rushed to the elevator and got on. Pushing the button for the fourth floor, the door closed. My heart was beating out my damn chest. I was nervous for what I was about to walk into. Making it to the door, I used the key to let us in.

"Oouu fuck, Ty, don't stop," I heard, and my ass lost it. The way she was moaning told me that he was giving her something that belonged to me. Anger took over me, and I charged at their ass. Tyrese didn't even see it coming.

"Kadeem, how to the fuck did you know I was here, and how the fuck did you get in?" he asked with his eyes bulging out is head. Caught in the motherfucking act, now he wanna switch that shit on me.

"Don't fuckin' worry about it. Is this the bitch that you been fuckin' to make you forget about our anniversary?" I asked, and he looked at me with sad eyes. His ass didn't have no right looking the way he did. "Your name must be

Sherry?" I asked her, and the bitch looked at me like I had grown two heads.

"No bitch, my name is Angelica, and you must be Kadeem. I've heard a lot about you, and the pictures didn't do any justice. I see why Ty won't leave your ass," she told me. Next thing I knew, I jumped on her ass and started rocking her to sleep. This bitch was fucking my man and pillow talking. Two ways to get her ass fucked up. I drug her ass until I was pulled off her by Shay.

"Ty might be your husband, but I have one up one you. I have his daughter," was the last thing I heard before I blacked out.

Chapter 1

Kadeem

"Damn, your ass need to hurry up, we gon' be late!" I hollered upstairs to my husband. I swear his ass would be late to his own damn funeral. If anything, I should have been the one to make us late.

"Hold up, damn Kadeem, I'm on my way down!" Tyrese yelled from upstairs, and I rolled my eyes.

He was taking me on a much-needed date. We were supposed to go out to dinner and come back home to watch movies. He was always busy, so the weekends were our time. We didn't have cellphones or anything because it was just about us. If you asked me, cellphones aren't needed on the weekends. They were only there to take away from our time.

Making his way downstairs, he looked good as shit. I could just eat his ass up. Shaking the thoughts out my head, I walked over and kissed him. That kiss sent chills down my spine and woke my lips between my legs up.

"It's about time your ass came down, it takes ya' ass entirely too long to get ready," I mentioned tohim, breaking the heated kiss. He looked at me and smirked. Ole sexy motherfucker.

"My fault, baby, you know a nigga like to get fresh for you." He licked my neck. That shit turned me on something serious. He knew that was my weakness, my knees buckled. I almost wanted to say fuck that, but I quickly shook the thought. We were going out even if I had other shit on my mind.

"Go on now, Tyrese, don't start no shit you can't finish," I told him, rushing to the door before he changed his mind.

"Oh, just remember whatever I start, I can finish," he whispered in my ear, and I felt my juices sliding down my legs.

This man just didn't know that I would have him in the corner sucking his thumb once I got finished with his ass. I ain't gon' brag, but this pussy would have you wanting to kill a nigga for looking at me wrong.

"Oh, hell naw, we have a date to go on. You already made us late, so come on." I pulled him by the arm. His ass was always on one.

Making it to the car, he made it to the passenger side to open the door for me; he was such a gentleman. I slid inside, and he closed the door.

"Thank you, baby, how am I so lucky to have a man like you?" I asked him as he made his way to his side. I wish this could last forever, it was just me and him. Nothing else mattered when we were together.

"You're welcome, baby, but I'm the lucky one." He winked at me before he started the car. My cheeks were hot as hell, Tyrese had that effect on me.

My baby looked so good tonight wearing a pair of acid washed jeans, a yellow Polo shirt, and some yellow and black J's. He was already light as hell, so the shirt complemented his skin tone. Tyrese was six-foot-five, two-hundred and twenty-five pounds solid, he kept his hair cut low. Baby, looking at his waves would make you sea sick. His body was always on point. He worked out seven days a week and watched what he ate. Tyrese was a rare breed, he never cheated on me or even looked at another female for all I knew. I was thankful for my baby and vice versa.

Making our way to Longhorn, Tyrese got out and came to open the door for me. He held out his hand for me to grab.

"Thank you, baby," I said as I grabbed ahold of his hand.

"Anything for my baby," he told me, kissing me on the lips.

Headed into the restaurant, he held the door open so I could walk in first.

"Damn baby, yo' ass lookin' fat." He walked up behind me, holding my waist. I loved when he complimented my figure, it only made me twist a little harder.

I couldn't get enough of this man. I don't care what anyone says, he can get it however he wants it.

"Thank you, daddy, you know I got you when we get home." I smirked at him. His freaky ass couldn't keep his hands off me and vice versa.

"Welcome to Longhorn's," one of the waitresses said.

"Reservations for Holly," Ty spoke as he was holding my waist.

"Yes sir, right this way." She headed over to our table, and we followed.

Getting to our booth, I slid in on one side, and he sat across from me. We started making small talk waiting for the server to come take our order. I couldn't wait to dig into the steak and potatoes. Just thinking about it made my mouth water.

"My name is Jenny, and I will be your server. What can I get you guys started to drink?" the preppy waitress asked us. Her ass was doing all this to get a tip. Hell, we might leave her a little something-something. That's only if she was like this the whole time we were here.

"We will have a glass of water with lemon, and I'll have a glass of Merlot. We would like to go ahead and order as well," I mentioned, and my husband nodded confirming what I had told her.

"Baby you know what you want?" I asked him, and I already knew he was gonna say a salad, but he shocked the hell out of me.

"I'll have a steak, medium well, with broccoli and a baked potato, no butter on my potato, and bring the A1 please." Damn, I didn't know my husband as well as I thought I did. I just kept looking at him in awe. My man had stepped his game up.

"I'll have a steak as well, well done please. Loaded bake potato and green beans. I would also like a side of barbeque sauce please," I explained, and she nodded. I was still looking at my husband.

"Very well, I'll have your drinks out shortly," she told us and left.

"When did you start eating steak? I was for sure you were gonna get a salad or some shit," I told him.

"See, you don't know your man as well as I know you. I knew what your ass was gonna get when you started. I know everything about your ass, Kadeem," he mentioned to me, and I blushed like a school girl. I just wondered why I didn't know his ass like he knew me.

We made small talk until our food came. When the food was sat at the table, we grabbed each other's hand and prayed. That was something we did before we ate anything, and I mean anything. After we prayed, we dug into our food. Our steaks were perfect, and my potato was everything that I could ask for. Finishing our dinner, I was stuffed. I couldn't wait to get home and snuggle up with my husband.

"Did y'all save room for dessert?" Jenny came back and asked us. I couldn't even answer fast enough, I knew that something nasty was about to fly out of Tyrese's mouth.

"I saved room for dessert, but mine is sitting across from the table," Tyrese disclosed, making me laugh. I swear his ass was something else, but he was all mine.

"Very well, here is your check, and you guys have a wonderful night," she told us, skipping off.

"I swear you are hell. Let's get out of here so you can get your dessert," I told him, and he licked his full set of lips. Those damn lips were so kissable, and I couldn't wait to feel them on my pussy lips.

When we were headed out the restaurant, my eyes locked with this tall, dark-skinned nigga. I mean, this nigga was fine as hell. Don't get me wrong, Tyrese was fine, but he was on a whole 'nother level. We kept eye contact until we made it out the door. Tyrese opened the door for me, but my mind was on this nigga in the restaurant. Something told me that this wasn't gonna be the last time we crossed paths.

Ahkeem

"Over here, baby!" Sherry snapped at me. Shawty was getting on my damn nerves. My mind was gone on shawty that left. Shawty was bad as fuck. She had the caramel complexion just like I like my women. If I looked at her long enough, I was scared I was gonna get a cavity.

"My bad, shawty, you 'bout ready to get out of here?" I asked her, and she sucked her teeth. She knew that I didn't do that disrespectful shit. "Fuck you suckin' your teeth for? Hold on, I got what you need, come on." I snatched her ass out the chair. I threw a couple hundreds on the table to cover our food and a tip.

Making it to the house, I unlocked the door and threw her ass on the wall. She loved all that rough shit. While I was kissing her, I was playing with her pussy, and that motherfucker was leaking. That let me know that she wanted it just as bad as I did. "This all you needed, huh?" I asked her.

"Yessss!" she moaned as her faucet started leaking. My nasty ass took my fingers out of her pussy and stuck them in my mouth. She had some good pussy and was my go to when I needed a good ass nut.

Releasing my dick, I turned her ass around and bent her over. I slid my dick up and down her wet box a couple times and rammed it in her pussy. I heard her gasp, that's what the fuck I wanted her to do. I don't know what came over me, but I started fucking the shit out of her. Not the normal fuck, but that rough shit. She tried to run, but I had a tight grip on her hair. Every time she ran, I pulled her back by her hair.

"Ahh, God damn, baby!" she screamed as I showed no mercy on her pussy.

"Take this dick, girl," I instructed, and she did just that. Her pussy was wetting a nigga up, a nigga felt like I was drowning.

"Fuck girl, you 'bout to make me bust," I informed her as I snatched my dick out her pussy and busted on her ass. Usually, we practiced safe sex, but tonight was different. I wanted to feel all that pussy around my dick.

Catching my balance, I walked into the bathroom and cleaned my dick off. Heading to my room, I grabbed some boxers and threw them on. Little mama from the restaurant had a nigga's mind going a mile a minute. She was fine as fuck, and the nigga she was hanging on to didn't hold a flame to me. He was occupying her until I was ready to make my move.

"Really nigga, that's how we do it now? Any other time you would clean me up after you got yourself together. What the fuck is really going on?" she asked me with her hands on her hips. I can't lie, Sherry was bad as fuck, but her mouth turned a nigga off.

"Go on somewhere with that shit, Sherry. You know what, call a cab and get the fuck out. I'll call you when I need some more pussy," I told her, dismissing her ass.

"Fuck you, Keem! You won't call me when you need some pussy because I'm not just a fuck. I'm better than that, and when you realize that, it's gonna be too late," she told me, and I looked at her ass like she was crazy.

"Fuck you mean, it's gonna be too late? Your ass ain't goin' nowhere, ya' ass is a thorn in a nigga's side. Fuck out of here with that shit. Have a good night, and I'll call you tomorrow." I lied. I was gonna be too busy doing research on the woman from the restaurant. Hopefully, I saw her ass again.

Sherry caught my drift, she got her shit and dipped. A nigga was glad because I wanted to sleep in peace tonight.

Plugging my phone up, I laid back in the bed and drifted off to sleep with little mama on my mind.

**

The next morning, I woke up to my fire alarm going off. I jumped up and grabbed my gun. Something told me to get up and check to make sure my door was locked after I kicked Sherry out last night, but a nigga was tired. Making it in the kitchen, I had my gun aimed at Sherry.
"Sherry, what the fuck you doin'? Burning my got damn house down." I boomed at her ass.

"I'm sorry, baby, last night we ended the night not on bad terms. I decided to get up and come over to cook for you. I turned the damn eye up too high, and this happened. I'm so sorry, baby," she told me, and I put my gun away. I threw whatever she was cooking out and let the windows up to get the smoke out. If I didn't get the alarm cut off soon, the damn fire department was gonna show up.

"Sherry, cooking is not for you. Stay the hell out my kitchen," I expressed to her, and she looked at me with sad eyes. "Come here, ma, I'm sorry, but you could have burned a nigga's house down. I'm not trying to be hard on you, but I ain't sugar coatin' shit either. You know how I am," I told her, kissing her forehead. The thing is, a nigga got a soft spot for Sherry. She'd been sticking by a nigga through it all, but she ain't wifey material. Sherry can't cook, she barely knew how to clean, but the pussy was phenomenal.

"What you got going on today?" She broke me out of my thoughts.

"I'ma head to the shop in a minute and make sure that things are running smoothly. I might hit the mall later on, what's up though?" I asked.

"I was just hoping that we could spend a little time together, that's all. I miss the days we would cuddle all day," she told me, and I chuckled not even meaning to.

"Sherry, not today," was all I said before I walked off. She was on the shits today, and I wasn't feeding into it.

Within an hour, I was pulling up to Keem's Car wash and Rims. I took pride in my shop, that's why I was there every day, even if it was only for an hour or two. I wasn't like most people that had business and was there only to collect the money. I was hands on with my business. Hell, I even washed a car here and there. It wasn't often, but still, I was there. Getting out the car, I spoke to everybody on the outside and headed inside the shop.

"Hey Julie, how is business today?" I asked.

"Hey boss, everything is good. We're making money, a little backed up, but nothing that we can't handle," she told me, and I nodded. That's what I wanted to hear.

"Good, I'm finna head to my office. If you need anything, don't hesitate to knock on my door," I told her, walking off.

When I walked in my office, I got right to work. I did payroll and ordered supplies for the shop. Once I was done, I decided to go out to see if the guys on the outside needed any help. I was glad I decided not to dress down today. Going outside, I spotted little mama from the restaurant, and look at God. She had been on my mind since I saw her ass. Walking over to her car, I tapped my knuckle on her window, and I think I scared her ass.

"What can I get for you today?" I asked her.

"I need the deluxe package, I'ma drop it off and pick it up later on," she told me, and I nodded.

"Ahkeem, but everyone calls me Keem." I stuck out my hand. She gladly took it.

"Kadeem is the government name, but everyone calls me Deem," she told me, and I was amazed.

"I'll take care of your car personally. Go get with Julie, give her your number, and I'll call you once I'm done. It was nice seeing you again, I'll call you once everything is taken care of." She nodded, and I couldn't help but think that God was answering my prayers.

Chapter 2

Kadeem

When I left the shop, I was shocked. I put two and two together and figured it was his shop. I didn't know that Ahkeem had so much going for himself. Looking at him, you wouldn't think he was an owner of his car wash. From looking at him, you would think he was in the street, but boy was I wrong. He had a good head on his shoulders, and I think that's what attracted me to his ass. Then when he talked to me, the gold shining in his mouth almost blinded a bitch. Yeah, he was gonna be a problem, I could already tell.

"Girl, what you over there cheesing so hard for? You must be over there texting Tyrese rock-head ass," my best friend, Shay, asked me. I looked at her ass sideways, she was always firing Tyrese up.

"Get off my husband! No, I was just thinking about this dude that I saw at Longhorn the other night, and then I see his ass today at the carwash. Bitch, I was star stuck, and he ain't even famous," I told her, and she cocked her head to the side.

"Bitch, I know I didn't hear your ass talkin' about another man. You know you worship the ground Tyrese ass walk on," she told me, and I laughed. That was so true, Tyrese was my everything.

We talked for a little longer, and we were on the way to the shop to get my car. When we pulled up to the shop, I jumped out. Shay crazy ass parked and got out. I swear this girl was hell. Walking inside the shop, Julie greeted me. Her spirit was the warmest I had seen in a long time.

"Coming to pick up your car, hold on, let me get boss man for you," she told me, and I gave her ass the side eye. Why did I need him to get my car? That had me puzzled.

"Julie, that's not necessary. Can't you just give me my keys, so I can be on my way?" I started, and she cut me off.

"Boss' orders. He told me to contact him once you showed up, I'm sorry. He is headed up from his office now," she told me, and Shay hit my arm.

"Oh yeah, I like her ass. She loyal," she whispered to me. I couldn't deal with them today.

"I'm glad to see you again. Your car is squeaky clean, and it's on the house," he started, but stopped. "Hey beautiful, Keem." He stuck out his hand for Shay to shake.

"Shay." She took his hand. "Can I get my car detailed too?" she asked, and he nodded. I couldn't do nothing but shake my head.

"Let me take you out. One friendly date, and that's it, I can see the rock on your finger. I ain't tryna break up a happy home, I'm just trying to be a friend," he told me, winking at me. I knew that he was lying, but I decided to take him up on that--under one condition.

"That's cool, but I need to bring Shay. That's the only way I can get away from my husband," I told him, looking him in the eyes.

"Oh, your nigga insecure. That's cool with me, I might have someone for Shay. I want your undivided attention," he told me, licking his lips. Damn, this man was fine as fuck!

"Ladies, have a good day, and Keem, I'll be contacting you for that date. Julie, thank you," he told us before he disappeared to the back.

"Bitch, I hope he got a brother. Homeboy is fine as fuck!" Shay asked me as soon as we made it outside.

"Girl, I dunno. Something is telling me that this is a bad idea, but shit, I only live once. I done had the same man my whole life. It's time to explore and see what the fuck happens." Shay was looking at me like she wanted to slap the shit out of me.

"Girl, do you, but don't get caught. Tyrese is a good man, and he is good to you," she reminded me. Ty was indeed good to me, but what would one date hurt?

We went our separate ways, and it was going on five o'clock. I knew I needed to get home to start on dinner before Ty got home from work. When I made it home, I took the chicken out the fridge and started cleaning it. I decided to make baked chicken and a salad for dinner tonight. Looking in the refrigerator, I saw that we were out of Ty's favorite dressing. I shot him a message and told him that I was gonna run and get some more. After telling me ok, I turned the chicken off and headed for the door. Cranking up the car, I pulled out the driveway. Driving a short distance, I pulled up to Kroger's. Grabbing my purse, I locked the car up and headed inside the store. Rushing to the salad dressing aisle, I grabbed the dressing and headed to the register. After paying for the dressing, I exited the store just as fast as I came in. It was now four-forty-five, I had about ten minutes to finish dinner and get it on the table. Pulling up at the house, I grabbed the dressing and made it into the house. After cutting the chicken and making Ty a plate, Ty was walking through the door.

"Damn baby, you got it smelling good as shit in here. Let me guess, you made my favorites, baked chicken breast and salad," he told me, walking over to me, kissing me on the forehead. "How was your day, baby?" he asked me as he released me.

"It was good, it's better now that you're home." I led him to the table with a smile.

"Baby, Shay and I are going out sometime next week," I informed him and waited for him to respond.

"That's cool, baby. Where y'all goin'?" he asked, and I shrugged.

"I dunno, we haven't gotten that part figured out yet. She thinks that I need to get out the house. I agree with her, though. I'm always stuck in here catering to you. Not that I mind, but I need to get out and have a good time," I told him, and he gave me the side eye.

"I mean, you sayin' it like I don't cater to your ass too. I make sure your ass straight too. Don't flip the script on me," he said, cutting his chicken. I didn't mean to piss him off, but I was only saying. "So, tell me what the fuck you mean by that?" he asked me, dropping his fork. I knew that this struck a nerve because I saw the veins in his forehead pulsing.

"I didn't mean anything by it, you know what, forget I even mentioned it. Go 'head and finish dinner." I just walked out of the kitchen. He was right on my heels, but I didn't even acknowledge his ass.

"So, that's how we do now? We can't talk about it, your ass be in your feelings and shit. It must be that time of the month because I swear that's the only time your ass act crazy," he told me before I walked into the room.

"Fuck you, Ty! Please leave me the hell alone right now. When I'm ready to talk to you, I will!" I snapped on his ass, slamming the room door and locking it. I knew I was wrong, but right now, I wanted to be alone.

***

Tyrese

I didn't know what the fuck Kadeem's problem was, but I was getting tired of her shit. Every time she got in one of her moods, she locked herself in the damn room. We're married, and shit didn't even feel like it. It was like her ass couldn't come to me and talk about me, her ass always beat around the bush. Her selfish ways and attitude was pising me off, and she was pushing me away.

"Kadeem, open the damn door and use your damn words. Stop acting like a little ass girl, you grown as fuck," I told her on the other side of the door.

"Ty, let me be right now. When I'm ready, we will talk. Right now, I'm going to bed," she told me, and I heard her flop in the bed.

"So, we really doin' this?" I asked her. When she didn't answer, I headed to the guest bedroom.

When I made it in the room, my phone dinged, indicating that I had a text message. Looking at the phone, I got frustrated. I didn't have time to deal with Angelica's shit today. Well, Angelica is my baby mother that Kadeem knows nothing about. Angelica stays in New York. Me and Angelica been messin' around since even before me and Kadeem got together. Angelica was good to a nigga, but she was on that other shit. We didn't want the same things. Her ass wanted the money but didn't want to work. Don't get me wrong, I loved my daughter, but her mother got on my last damn nerve. She always threw it up in my face saying that she was gonna tell my wife about our daughter. I catered to her every need so that she wouldn't do that. I paid over five-thousand dollars in child support, and I took business trips up there to see them. I was missing my daughter's life, and I hated it, but she understood that her dad loved her and would do anything for her. If Kadeem ever found out about them, I know for a fact that she would leave my ass. Angelica knew that shit, and I that's why her ass texted me so much. Kadeem and I have separate accounts, so she knew nothing about what I did with my coins. She probably would be all in my shit if she knew how much I spent on them, but that was a story for another day.

Fred: When are we gonna see you? It's been a while.

Me: I'll be making a trip up there next week. I'll text you when I touch down. How is my daughter?

Fred: She is as well as expected when her father isn't in her life. Why don't you stop playing and come be with us?

Me: Naw I'm good, like I said, I'll call you when I touch down. Don't text back.

Angelica and I had an understanding. When I said something, she did that shit. That's why when I went to New York, I broke her off with some dick. Getting myself together, I laid in the bed. I tried to text Kadeem, but her ass didn't text back. After getting comfortable in the bed, I drifted off to sleep.

Wifey: I'm sorry about last night. I didn't mean to make it seem like you didn't take care of me. I love you, and I will always love you.

After reading the message, I laid my phone beside me and hopped up out the bed. After handling my hygiene, I threw on some clothes and headed to the kitchen. Making it there, Deem had my coffee and blueberry muffin waiting for me. My wife was bomb as fuck, but that damn attitude she had be turnin' a nigga off. I sat down at the table and tried to enjoy my coffee and muffin. It was cut short to a nagging wife.

"Ty, you really gon' sit in here and not acknowledge that I'm even standing here?" she nagged.

"Oh, hey baby, I didn't even see you standing over there," I lied, and she sucked her teeth.

"Cut the bull shit, baby, I said I was sorry. Please don't do this." She pouted.

"I forgive you. Next time, I'ma have to tap that ass," I told her, slapping her on the ass.

"Baby, don't tempt me with a good time. Go ahead and get ready for work. I got you when you get home tonight," she told me, and my dick jumped. My wife had that kinda effect on a nigga.

After what seemed like forever, I was dressed and ready to leave out for work. I loved what I did, but I wanted more. I made an honest living, and I made sure Kadeem was good before anything. I wasn't rich, but I damn sholl had enough money to last for a little bit. I was the owner of Rese Trash Company. My company picked up on Mondays and Fridays. The rest of the week, we sat in the office trying to come up with different ideas for the company. I wanted to expand, but I didn't want to relocate.

Getting to the office, I walked in and got straight to work. I had so much shit to do and so little time. Next week, I was going to New York to handle some business. I needed to make sure that my wife would be straight while I was gone. That's why I needed to give her this act right to continue to make her feel she was the only one. After finishing up my busy day, I made it home to my wife. With all the shit we were going through, I didn't forget about her. Even when her ass wanted to act a fool.

****

Today was the day that I left to go to New York, I wasn't ready for this shit. Deem had been in her feelings, and I couldn't deal with her ass right now.

"Baby, why can't I go with you?" she whined. "I just wanna spend time with you, baby."

"I already told you this trip is for work not play. When I come back, I'll take you anywhere you wanna go, deal?"

"Anywhere?" she mocked. Her eyes lit up like a kid on Christmas Day.

"Baby, the world is yours, where ever you wanna go. I gotta be getting on the road. I'll call you when I make it to New York," I told, her kissing her all over her face. I hated that I had to lie to her, but if I told her the truth, she would probably leave my ass. That's why I did any and everything to keep her happy.

"Alright baby, be careful, I love you," she mentioned to me. I kissed her one last time, and I headed out the door.

The drive there was a long and boring one, but I was thankful that I made it there in one piece. The first place that I went when I made it there was my baby mom's spot. Damn, I didn't pay attention, but they were living good as fuck. After parking my car, I grabbed my phone and called Kadeem.

"Hello," she answered groggy.

"Hey baby, I was just calling you to let you know I made it here. I'm finna get me a shower and call it a day," I lied.

"Well baby, I'm glad you made it. Get some rest and make sure you call me tomorrow. Love you."

"I love you too, girl. I'ma call you as soon as I wake up in the morning," I uttered to her before ending the call.

Powering my phone off, I placed it in the glove box and headed in the house. When I made it to the door, it was quiet as hell in there. Hell, it was almost midnight; I would hope they were sleep. Letting myself in, I closed and locked the door behind me. I missed my little family, and I was about to wake them up. Daddy needed some attention! Walking through the house, I smiled because I knew that the money that I sent wasn't going to waste. Walking closer in the house, I saw that our bedroom light was on. That told me that Angelica was still up.

"Daddy!" Angel screamed as soon as she spotted me.

"What up, baby girl. Did you miss daddy?" I asked, and she nodded her head up and down fast. I swear she was the air that a nigga breathed. "Why you ain't sleep though?" I asked.

"Mommy told me that I cold stay up to see you come in. When are you gonna move up here with Mommy and I?" she asked me, and I was feeling bad as shit. She shouldn't have to worry about that, and I should be here for her.

"Don't worry, daddy will be here for you soon. I just need to take care of business back home. How about I send for you to come visit me?" I asked her, and she nodded. "Go ahead and get in bed so I can talk to Mommy real quick," I told her, putting her down.

"Promise me that you'll be here in the morning when I wake up," she told me, putting out her little pinky. I looped my pinky with hers.

"I promise, baby girl. I love you, now go get some sleep. Look at those bags under your eyes," I gave her my word before tickling her.

"Enough, Daddy." She snorted. After putting her down and leaving out the room, Angelica started.

"Why would you lie to her like that? You know damn well you not gon' send for her, you don't want your little secret out. You don't want your little wife to know what's really going on," she damn near yelled at me.

"Calm ya' ass down. If I send for her, you best believe she comin'. I could care less what my wife say, she can love her or hit the road. Simple as that," I warned her, snatching her ass up. "I got what you need though, since you wanna act up. Assume the position," I boomed, and she did as I asked. "Let me go check on Angel first, and I'ma get you right," I mention, adjusting my hard on in my pants. I heard her smack her lips, but I didn't care.

Walking in Angel's room, she was knocked out. Her little body was thrown all over the bed. I laughed as I walked over to her and threw the blanket over her. After kissing her on the forehead, I exited her room, closing the door behind me. Making it back to our room, Angelica was in the bed with her legs open wide. Her pretty pussy was glistening from her juice. I walked over to her and grabbed her ankles and pulled her to the edge of the bed. Her pussy was looking right, but the only pussy I ate was my wife. Call me what you want.

"You ready for this?" I asked her, teasing her with my dick.

"Fuck yes," she moaned, and that shit made my dick harder.

"Let me in, baby," I ordered her, pushing into her tight pussy. I could tell that she wasn't givin' another nigga my pussy by how tight it was. After getting all the way in, I started fucking her insides up.

"Oh, my God, Tyrese, I missed you so much!" she screamed as I was beating her pussy up.

"Whose pussy is this?" I asked, slowing down before I busted.

"Yours, all yours, baby," she cooed before her body started to shake. That's how I knew that she was cumming. I sped up my pace and busted right along with her.

"Fuck girl, why your shit gotta be so good?" I asked her.

"Better than wifey?" she asked, and I looked at her ass like she was crazy.

"Never better than wifey, but y'all running neck and neck," I lied as I busted in her ass.

After taking a shower, I got my ass in bed. A nigga was tired as hell, and I knew that today was gonna be an eventful day with the family. As soon as my head hit the pillow, a nigga was counting sheep.

Chapter 3

Kadeem

"So, you tryna tell me that you asked him to go with him, and he told you no?" Shay asked me, and I nodded. Shay and I were sitting in the living room drinking wine, catching up.

"I mean, I don't know what's going on. Then I called him this morning, and it went straight to voicemail. Ty never gave me a reason to think he was cheating on me, but now, I don't know," I mentioned to her, and my phone dinged. I was hoping that it was Ty, but it was Ahkeem. He wasted no time, and I liked his determination.

Shay: Dinner and movie today?

Me: Sure, we're over here bored out our mind. What movie are we going to see?

Shay: Whatever you wanna watch. I just wanna spend time with you.

Me: Cool, tell me what time we need to meet you there and we'll be there.

Shay: Meet me at this address at 3. Wear a dress and no panties.

"What you over there laughin' at?" Shay broke me out of my thoughts.

"Ahkeem said meet us at this address at three, and then his ass told me to wear a dress with no panties. I hope his ass don't think I'ma give the cookie up just like that. Hell, I don't know; if he acts right, I just might," I informed her, and she cocked her head to the side.

"Bitch, look at you. Come down off that high horse, let's not forget you're married," she warned me, and I instantly started feeling bad. Shit, if Ty could do him, I could do me.

"It's not even like that. He's just a friend, and that's it," I told her, getting up from the couch and heading to the kitchen. Shay did have a good point, but hey, he wanted to act single, so could I.

"I'm finna get out of here. I'll be back about two-thirty, and I'm only going to make sure you don't do something you will regret," she drilled me, and I laughed. Her ass was hell, but I loved her no doubt.

"You can come, but I don't need you cock-blocking. I mean, if he play his cards right, I might just lift my dress. Easy access, you know I won't be wearing any drawls," I uttered, and she shook her head.

"Do you, bitch, but keep me out of it when you get caught." She shrugged, and I waved her off.

After Shay left, I went upstairs and picked out my dress for tonight. I didn't even bother with picking out panties. I know I'm happily married, but when your spouse doesn't show you that attention, then it is what it is. I wasn't finna intentionally sleep with Ahkeem, but if it led to it, then that's what it was gonna be. After calling Ty and getting the voicemail one last time, I threw my phone on the bed and fell right beside it. I didn't know I was so tired until I hit the pillow though. Ty was stressing me the hell out, and I didn't know what to do.

It seemed like I was just closing my eyes when my phone started ringing off the hook. Looking at it, I got instantly pissed. I just wondered what his ass wanted, since I'd been calling his ass all day and he was just now returning my damn call. *"Yeah,"* I answered the phone.

"Dang, is that a way to answer the phone for your husband?" he asked, and I sucked my teeth.

"I been callin' your black ass all day, and you wanna just now call me. What the fuck you were doing so important that you had to turn your phone off?" I asked, peeping his game.

"Take some of that bass out your voice when you talkin' to me. I was handling business today, that's why the fuck my phone was turned off!" He snapped on me. *"Your period must've started, I swear yo' ass be doin' the most when it's about to come on."*

"Ty, save that shit for someone that believe that shit. Game peep game. As many times as you went to New York, you never turned your phone off, so please don't come at me with that bullshit. If I wasn't crazy, I would think that your ass had a whole 'nother family in New York," I questioned him, and the line got quiet. That gave me what I needed to know.

"Deem, you trippin', I don't have time to put up with your shit. A nigga out here makin' money moves, and your ass wanna say that a nigga cheatin'. Don't even offend me like that. You know all I want is your mean ass," he revealed, making me blush. I started to text Ahkeem and cancel our date, but what could one friendly date do?

"I hear you, baby. Let me get back to my nap, I'll call you once I get up. I love you," I spoke right before I ended the call.

I woke up to Shay's big mouth ass. I couldn't sleep for shit around this bitch. Rolling out of the bed, I went in the bathroom and handled my hygiene. After finishing in the bathroom, I made my way back in the room and grabbed my phone. Ahkeem had texted me to make sure I was still coming today, and I wouldn't miss it for nothing in the world. I needed some kind of fun in my life.

"Damn, it's about time that your ass woke up. I been out here for about forty-five minutes looking crazy," Shay informed me, and I laughed at her ass.

"Girl, I was trying to get my beauty sleep, and guess who the fuck figured out that he had a wife at home?"

"Tyrese finally called your ass. I swear y'all be doin' the most. Why you do that man like that? You know that he workin' hard so your ass doesn't have to," she advised, and I nodded.

"Then when we were on the phone, I told him that it was like he got a family in New York, and the line got quiet. I swear if his ass is cheating on me, I will chop his dick off and feed it to him," I vented to her.

"Bitch, Tyrese ain't that damn crazy. He knows that your ass doesn't got it all. The fuck he would mess up for?" She assured me, but something was telling me different.

"Whatever. What are you wearin' today?" I asked, changing the subject.

"I have a cute little body suit and some heels. What about you?" she asked.

"Bitch, you already know what I'm wearing, I just hope my pussy don't fail me," I told her sighing. "Come on, we got like forty-five minutes to get dressed and make it to the address," I announced, before rushing to my room to shower and get ready.

About thirty minutes later, we were dressed and heading to the car. For some reason, I was nervous as hell. Something told me that this was a bad idea, but I pushed that to the back of my head. While Shay was driving, I decided to text my husband to see what he was up to.

Me: Hey baby, what you up to? Me and Shay about to go out to eat and catch a movie.

Hubby: Handling business, baby, I'll call you once I get done.

I decided not to text back. I wanted to turn off my phone, but then again, I didn't want to miss an important call. When we pulled up to the house, my nerves were trying to get the best of me. I wanted to turn around and take my ass home, but Shay wasn't finna let that happen.

"You might as well come on. Your ass dragged me out the house, don't be nervous now," Shay reminded me, and I cocked my head to the side.

"OI naw, bitch, I didn't put a gun to your head and make you come out. You told me that you were coming to make sure I didn't do anything that I might regret. So make sure you do just that. Now, come on, bitch, before I change my mind," I confessed, jumping my ass out the car before she could jump bad with me.

"Welcome ladies, you must be Kadeem and Shay. Come right this way, Ahkeem and Hakeem are waiting for you. Oh, where are my manners, my name is Bonney," she greeted us, and we followed behind her.

"It's about time y'all made it, I thought you was gon' stand a nigga up," Ahkeem told us, showing his mouth full of gold.

"I see you listened to me," he informed me, whispering in my ear. Lawd, this man was doing something to me.

"Shay, this is my brother, Hakeem. Hakeem, this is Shay," he introduced the two, and his brother was just as cocky as he was. I knew they were gonna hit it off just fine.

"The pleasure is all mine. Damn, you got a fat ass," he mentioned, and I laughed because I knew she was finna read this nigga.

"Nigga, if you don't get your dick beaters off me. You don't know me to be touching me on the ass. I don't know who the fuck you take me to be," Shay read his ass, and I couldn't do nothing but laugh.

"Damn, my bad, little baby, it ain't even that serious. Come on before we miss the movie!" He snapped on her.

Ahkeem took my hand and led me to a room. The theater room, by what it looked like, I was impressed. I knew that he had it all, but baby, I didn't know he had it like this.

"Damn, this is dope," I announced, hyped.

"Calm down, ma, it ain't that serious. I'm glad you like it. Have you figured out what you wanna watch yet?" he asked me, and I looked around for Shay.

"Let's watch *Widows*, I heard it was a good movie," I beamed, and he nodded.

"Play *Widows*," he called out, and *Widows* popped on the screen.

We got comfortable in the middle section and watched the movie. During the movie, I stole a couple of glances at him, and he did the same thing. Ahkeem had his arm around me, and it felt so good, that was until my phone rung. My husband was calling, but I wasn't finna disrespect Ahkeem like that.

"Ah, tell that nigga you will call him back tonight, that's if I don't put your ass to sleep," he mentioned to me as I crossed my legs.

Me: Shay and I are out. I'll call you when I make it to the house.

I texted him and turned my phone off. I wanted him to see how I felt when I was constantly calling him and got no response. I knew this was an argument waiting to happen, but I would take that when it came.

"Oh, my God, that movie was amazing, and I'm starving,"

"Yeah, it was good, best friend!" I heard Shay yell, but I didn't see her ass.

"Come on, let me feed ya'," Ahkeem told me, helping me up out the chair and wrapping his hand around my waist. Lawd, please keep me near the cross.

"What are we eating?" I asked.

"Whatever on the menu you want, we eatin'," he told me, showing me to the dining room.

Whie goig into the kitchen, Ahkeem pulled out my chair and waited for me to sit before walking around to his side and sitting down. I had a taste for Lasagna and salad, something simple but filling. While Bonney was preparing the food, Ahkeem and I got to know each other a little better. As we talked, I figured out Ahkeem was a sweet heart. Under that hard demeanor, Ahkeem was a teddy bear.

One thing led to another, and next thing I knew, my dress was being pulled up, and I was bussing it wide open for

Ahkeem. Now, this was so wrong, but it felt so right as he pounded in my wetness.

"Aahhhh, oh, my God, fuck! That's my spot!" I cried to Ahkeem, and it fell on deaf ears.

"That's what I'm talking about, throw that ass back," he instructed, and I did just that. Lawd, I can't believe this man was doing shit to my body that my husband didn't do.

"Fuck, I'm cumming!" I cried as I wet his dick up.

"Let that shit go, baby. I can tell that your husband ain't doin' it right, look how I got that body cummin'," he informed me as I was releasing again. "Fuck!" I screamed.

"That's right. Let that shit go. Can I cum in you?" he asked.

"Yesssss!" I screamed, not realizing what I had done until I felt his dick thumping inside of me.

"I gotta go," I confessed, pulling my dress down. I knew I needed to get the fuck away from his ass. I didn't even know this man like this, and I was letting him cum inside me. I had to be one of the stupidest bitches out here.

Making it outside to the car, I powered back on my phone, and I had all kinds of missed calls and text messages from my husband. From the looks of thing, he was mad as fuck. Calling Shay, I waited for her to pick up the phone.

"Bitch, we gotta go."

"Shay unavailable right now. Leave her, and I'll make sure she gets home safe," Hakeem mentioned, but I wasn't leaving without Shay.

"Naw, I can't do that. We came together, and we're leaving together. Put Shay on the phone," I damn near screamed into the phone.

"I'm on my way out," she uttered and hung up in my face. Something told me that when I made it home, it wasn't gonna be good.

"Hey baby, what you doin'?" I asked as soon as he picked up the phone.

"Deem, where the hell you been? I been callin' yo' ass all damn day, and the bitch went straight to voicemail."

"Shay and I was at dinner, and my phone went dead. I forgot to charge it earlier, I'm sorry, baby," I quickly lied.

"Where y'all at now? Let me talk to Shay," he demanded, and I panicked because Shay hadn't made it out yet.

"Hang on, she comin' out the bathroom now. Here Shay, Ty wants to talk to you," I said out loud as she was walking to the car. Her ass was walking a little too slow for my liking.

"Hey Ty, what's up? Sorry about that. I told Deem to call you off my phone, but she told me that she was gonna call you as soon as she got in the car to put her car on the charger. Yeah, we went to Olive Garden and went to see Widows. Yeah, we headin' to the house now," she lied with a straight face. And y'all see why I fucks with Shay the long way, she had my back and vice versa.

"Alright baby, I love you, and I'll talk to you when I make it home," I said to him before ending the call.

"Bitch, that was a close one. Tyrese sounded mad as hell, but he calmed down once I confirmed everything. Tell me what the fuck happened in there and why you ran out so quick?"

"One thing led to another, and my damn dress was pulled up. Ahkeem did things to my body that my husband never did, bitch, and to top everything off, I let his ass cum in me like I wasn't a married woman. I feel dirty, and I don't know if his ass has something or not. He said one date, and that's it. I'm not finna keep fuckin' with him, although the dick was bomb as fuck," I vented to her in one breath.

"I know you lyin', Deem, I know your ass is smarter than that. Did your ass even go to the bathroom to piss the nut out?" she asked me, and I shook my head no. "Hoe, ya' ass is stupid. Let's go to the Walmart and get you a Plan B. You better hope that this nigga is clean, or that's your ass," she told me as the water works started.

On the way to Walmart, the only sounds being heard throughout the car was me sniffling. I was scared shitless of what was about to happen. When we made it to Walmart, I let Shay run in and get the Plan B. My mind was all over the place.

Shay: Damn, I didn't dick you down right or something? Your ass just dipped on me. What's really going on?

Me: I think it's best for us to go our separate ways. You asked for one date, and I gave that to you. Have a nice life.

Shay: If that's what you wanna do, then so be it, but I'm pretty sure you loved that shit just as much as I did.

I erased his number out my phone and got myself together. I had a whole husband at home, and I was carrying on like I was single. Shay jumped back in the car and threw me the box in my lap. I had a bottle of water from earlier and threw the pill in my mouth. There was no way in hell I was finna have a baby on my husband like that. I mean, even if he was doing the same, I still couldn't do him like that. First thing in the morning, I was getting my ass up and heading to the clinic to get tested, and I prayed that everything came back negative.

"I'ma stay at your house tonight, I'll get up in the morning and go home," Shay informed me, breaking me out my thoughts.

"That's cool with me, I don't want to be alone anyways. All of this is too much for me. Here I was catching feeling for this man, I barely knew him," I told her, and I heard her gasp.

"Bitch no, say it ain't so. Ya' ass is happily married, so I thought. I mean, what you gon' do?"

"I'ma see how Ty acts when he comes home, I just don't know," I told her, walking in the house. Turning on the light, Ty was sitting on the chair and scared the shit out off me. I didn't know what to do, I still had this stranger's nut on me, and the dress that I had on wasn't for a married woman. *Fuck, think quick, Kadeem.*

Chapter 4

Tyrese

"Hey wifey, you don't look happy to see your man. Sup Shay, Kadeem is finna go to bed. She'll holla at you tomorrow," I told her, but Shay didn't budge. She just looked between me and Kadeem.

"Naw, I'm tired, so I'm staying tonight," she informed me, getting comfortable on the couch. She was ignoring the death stare I was giving Kadeem. To say I was pissed was an understatement, I was livid.

"Did you have a good time with, what club did y'all go to? It's no way in hell that a married woman goes out like this," I mentioned with a look of disgust.

"Hey, baby. I didn't know you were coming home so soon. If I would have known, I would have cooked dinner. Shay and I had a good time. Ain't that right, Shay?" She looked at Shay for help. Little did she know, I peeped her game when she walked in.

"Yeah, it was ok, I wished we would have chosen something else, and I think that pasta torn my stomach up," she told her before she rushed off to the bathroom.

"So, you really not gon' show your man no love?" I asked her with my hands out. She looked scared as hell, that's how I knew that my assumptions were true.

"Baby, give me a minute, you know I got you." She winked nervously.

We had all the time in the world. If she was going to the bathroom, I was going too.

She walked into the bathroom and tried to close the door, and I stopped her by placing my foot in the door. We'd been married for four years, and she ain't never did no shit like this before.

"Handle your business," I told her, and she nervously pulled her dress up.

It pissed me off even more to see that she didn't have no panties on. Like, did she leave the house like that, or did they magically disappear? After she was done, she flushed and turned the shower on. Lifting the dress over her head, I admired all her curves. As mad as I was, my dick still stood to attention when it came to Kadeem. I started undressing, shit, I was finna get in too.

"Baby, what you doin'?" She asked me nervously.

"I'm finna get in and get some of that sweet pussy. Fuck you mean, what I'm doin'?" I snapped at her ass. She was really pissing me the fuck off, but my dick never went limp.

"I'm not in the mood right now, I just wanna wash the movies and Olive Garden off me," she mentioned before stepping in the shower. A nigga was 38 hot, she ain't never did no shit like this. I paced the floor trying to get my thoughts together. I knew that I was doing dirty, but I can't handle that shit being done to me. Next thing I knew, I pulled the curtains back and grabbed her by the throat.

"You been givin' my pussy away? I swear to God, I'll kill you and that nigga. Play with me if you want to," I told her as she clawed my hand. I didn't realize how tight my grip was until she started turning blue in the face, and I released her. "I'm sorry, baby, I don't know what came over me. Forgive me, I swear it won't happen again," I informed her, not believing my damn self.

"Ty, get out," she told me above a whisper, but I wasn't leaving her like this. "Ty, get the fuck out!" she screamed as the tears soaked her face. Damn, a nigga fucked up big time!

"Baby, I'm sorry, please don't leave me," I begged.

"Best friend, everything ok in there?" Shay hollered through the other side of the door.

I felt defeated. I grabbed my duffle bag and started filling it up with clothes. I didn't have to take this shit, I had another family in New York that needed me. After packing up as much as possible, I push past Shay and headed out the door. I was gonna stay at the hotel until I figured shit out. I knew for a fact that Kadeem had stepped out on me. Her body language and the way that she couldn't look at me in the face told me, and the fact that I wasn't man enough to walk away hurt me. Never in life had I laid a hand on Kadeem, but she pushed me to the limit tonight.

After making it to the hotel and getting settled, I smoked me a couple of blunts to ease my mind. The more I smoked, the hornier a nigga got. I didn't want just any pussy though, I wanted to slide inside my wife. Seeing that wasn't gonna happen, I grabbed my phone and hit up one of my jump offs. When she told me that she was on the way, I went inside the bathroom to freshen up. Just as I was stepping out, there was a knock at the door. Naked as the day I was born, I opened the door and let Sheryl in. She looked down at my dick, and it was standing at full attention. Closing the door, she got down on her knees and got to work. This was so wrong, but it felt so right.

"Fuck Sheryl, you better suck this dick," I moaned out like a little bitch. She was deep throating my shit like her life depended on it. A couple minutes later, I was spilling my seed deep down her throat. "Fuck, thanks for that," I told her, snatching my dick out of her mouth.

"Ty, stop being selfish and let me ride that dick," she demanded as I laid on the bed.

After positioning herself on my dick, she started bouncing on the dick. I had forgotten that Sheryl was a freak in the sheets. She quickly reminded me. Grabbing her left breast, I popped it in my mouth and gently sucked on it.

"Ouuu shit, Ty, suck 'dem titties, baby," she moaned as she threw her head back. After giving the right one the same attention, I felt her explode on my dick.

"Ride through that shit, ma." I popped her on the ass, and she did just that. "Thanks for the pussy, ma, you can let yourself out," I revealed, dismissing her.

Sheryl knew her place; she grabbed her shit and got ghost. That's why I didn't mind breaking her off from time to time. After cleaning my dick off, I fell on the bed with my eyes closed. Today was a trying day, but tomorrow was gonna be a better day!

***

Kadeem

"What the fuck happened in here? I know that Ty didn't put his hands on you, I know his ass ain't that crazy. Call that nigga and tell him to come the fuck back and put his hands on me, I dare his ass!" Shay snapped. I was still in disbelief that Ty put his hands on me, and I didn't even do shit.

"Shay, it's cool, I deserved that. I couldn't lay down with him when I just fucked Ahkeem," I told her honestly.

"Bitch, I still can't believe you slept with a man you just met. What in the hell were you thinking?" she asked me, not making the matter any better. "That still don't give him no right to put his hands on you. Tell me all about it though," she demanded.

"I ain't even gon' lie, his dick game was phenomenal. He was doing things to my body that Ty doesn't do. I mean, I felt bad about cheating on Ty, so I jumped my ass up and left. Ahkeem is a great man, and I'm sure he can have any woman that he wants," I vented, feeling myself getting sad.

"Tell me you ain't catchin' feelings this early. Y'all just met."

"So what we just met? It's something there, and I feel it. I know his ass felt it too," I informed her, and she popped my forehead.

"Bitch, wake the fuck up. Ahkeem did all that shit to get in your pants. I can't believe you slept with him."

"Ya' ass can't talk, I know you busted it wide open for Hakeem," I told her, and she blushed

"It different, I'm single as a dollar-bill, baby. You got a whole husband, what the hell is wrong with you?"

"I dunno, I was wanting to try something different, and it was so worth it," I told her honestly.

Unknown: I want you to know that I can't stop thinking about your ass. It's something about you that I can't shake, and I know your ass feel it too.

Me: I'm married, I can't do this. I don't care how much I enjoyed it, it can't happen again. Please don't make things difficult.

Unknown: I don't give a damn about you being married, I want you.

"Bitch, why you over there blushin'? That must be him?" she asked, snatching my phone. "Oh, hell naw, bitch, you ain't finna use me. Save that nigga number under somebody else name," she told me, throwing my phone back at me.

"Shay, I dunno what to do. There's a spark there, but it's hard to explain. You wouldn't understand unless you were in my shoes," I told her, dropping my head.

"Naw, lift your head up. All jokes aside, remember your vows. Don't let ten minutes of pleasure cost you your marriage. If you don't wanna be with Ty anymore, end it before you step into something else," Shay told me, and I nodded.

She was right, I went ahead and blocked Ahkeem out my mind. I had to work on my marriage. Tyrese was a good man, and that's why I married his ass. The rest of the night, Shay and I talked and ate pizza. I was glad that I had a friend like her. We cut up, but she put my ass in line when she needed to. We ended up falling asleep in the middle of White Chicks.

The next morning, I was woken up with my phone vibrating off the hook. It seemed like I just laid my ass down. Grabbing my phone, I hit the green button and put it up to my ear.

"I'm sorry about last night, baby. Please don't leave me," Ty begged.

"I'm not leaving you, but I need a break from you right now. You have never put your hands on me, nor have you talked to me the way you did," I told him, and the line got quiet.

"Deem, I'll give you all the space you need, but I have one question. Did you fuck that nigga?" he asked. That question threw me off guard. How did he even know I was with a nigga?

"Ty, what nigga are you talking about? I told you that me and Shay went out. What, you don't believe me?"

"Hell naw, the shit you had on told me otherwise. You had on that fuck me dress, and I peeped how you didn't have no drawls on. So, you can tell that lie to someone that don't know yo' ass!" He snapped at me. *"Where did I go wrong, and how can I fix it? I love you, Kadeem, and this marriage is till death do us part,"* he mentioned calmly. The way he said till death do us part sent chills down my spine.

"I hear you, Ty. I'm finna get up and get my day started. I'll talk to you later," I revealed to him ending the call.

"Bitch, can you be quiet?" Shay asked, pulling the pillow over her head.

"Hoe, you in my room, I can talk as loud as I want," I told her, pulling the pillow from over her head. "I'm finna cook breakfast, you want some?" I asked her, heading to the bathroom to handle my hygiene.

As I sat on the toilet, I felt the soreness between my legs. That reminded me of Ahkeem; this was gonna be harder than I thought to get him out my mind. I felt myself comparing him to my husband. Where Ty just liked to do the basic positions, Ahkeem liked to choke me and slap my ass. I can't even lie, I loved every moment that I spent went him. After relieving my bladder, I wiped and flushed the toilet. Moving to the sink, I washed my hands and brushed my teeth. Looking in the mirror, I saw a glow that I'd never seen before. Ty made me happy, but Ahkeem made me glow like this.

"Deem, come get this damn phone, it's been blowing the hell up over here. Loverboy just ain't givin' up on you," she told me, throwing me my phone.

Unknown: Kadeem, I can't live without you. Please don't make me.

Me: Keem, please don't do this.

Unknown: So, you tellin' me you didn't enjoy it as much as I did? I feel something that I never felt before. Don't act like you don't.

Me: It's not about enjoying it. I can't deny that your sex game is great, but I am a married woman.

Unknown: You wasn't saying that shit when I was beating that shit up. Let me take you out to lunch.

I can't deny Ahkeem had my nose wide open, but I wasn't about to feed into his cockiness. I was gonna try to work things out with my husband, and the only way I could do that is if I forgot about him completely. I dialed the 1-800 number for Verizon to change my number. After I got my new number, the first person I texted was my husband.

Me: Hey baby, what you doin'?

It took him a minute to text back, but I didn't think anything of it. I got up and made Shay and I some breakfast. Today, I wasn't doing a thing; I was laying around the house trying not to think of Ahkeem. As I got started on breakfast, my phone dinged. I knew that it was nobody but my husband, but I wasn't ready for the response that I saw.

Hubby: Who the fuck is this?

You know I was finna play with him and see if he told on himself.

Me: Oh, you don't remember me now. You weren't saying that when you was deep inside my ocean last night.

Hubby: Sherry?

What the fuck, I wondered who the fuck Sherry was. I know that I shouldn't have been playing, but I didn't think that he would go out and cheat on me. The tears started falling, and I let out a scream. I knew that I didn't deserve this shit. One slip up and his ass went and stuck his dick in another bitch. Now I feel bad for cutting Ahkeem off, but if he wanted to play, two could play this game.

Chapter 5

Ahkeem

I had been calling Kadeem with no answer. Then the last time I called her, I saw that she switched her number on a nigga. I felt myself getting angry, but I don't know why. I knew that her ass was married, and I was cool with that, but after I got that pussy, all that shit changed. I didn't want her with another man, not even her husband. This shit was crazy; my ass was always falling for the married one, but it was something about that married pussy that I couldn't get off my brain.

"Nigga, what yo' ass over there thinkin' about? Ya' ass in deep thought too," Hakeem told me, laughing.

"Man, I can't get shawty off my brain, and then her ass up and changed her number on a nigga. That shit fuckin' with me," I expressed to him honestly.

"You know I can find her ass for you, all you gotta do is say the word," he told me, and I nodded. Hakeem was a nerd and could find anybody in the USA.

"I know it, bruh. I'ma let her ass come back to her senses. She'll be back, I know that her husband can't do the shit I can to her body," I told him. Call me cocky, and I might just own up to it.

"Shit, come on, let's smoke this blunt. Yo' ass need this bitch," he told me, tossing me the blunt.

He ain't never lied. As soon as the smoke hit my lungs, it relaxed a nigga. My brother and I talked and smoked the rest of the day away. I didn't feel like going to the carwash, so I didn't. That was the beauty of being a business owner; I didn't have to go in if I didn't want to. As I was laying in the bed, I came up with a bright idea; if I couldn't have Kadeem, I would go with the next best thing, Sherry. After texting her and her telling me that she was on the way, I got up and handled my hygiene before she came. While in the shower, Kadeem flashed across a nigga's brain, and I quickly shook her out. She made it clear that she didn't want shit else to do with my ass. Washing and rinsing a couple time, I jumped my ass out the shower, just as the doorbell rung. Wrapping the towel around my waist, I headed to the door. Snatching it open, Sherry was standing there with lust in her eyes.

"It's about time your ass made it, I thought you was gon' stand a nigga up," I told her, pulling her in the house.

"Now you know I wouldn't pass up on no good dick," she told me, releasing the towel from my waist. She wasted no time swallowing my dick whole. Sherry was a certified head doctor. When I wanted toe curling head game, she was the one I called.

"Sherry, you better suck that dick, girl," I told her, grabbing a fist full of her weave.

"Fuck Ty, you taste so good," she moaned, and I snatched my dick out her mouth.

"Who the fuck you call me, bitch?" I asked her, throwing her against the wall. As long as we been fuckin', she never called me another nigga's name. That shit did something to me like it made me a whole 'nother nigga.

"What are you talking about? I called you Keem," she told me, looking scared.

"You a damn lie, who the fuck is Ty?" I spat at her ass. Not that I cared, I just felt disrespected.

"Ty is someone that I been messin' with from time to time. He's married and when they have problems, he always calls me," she told me, shaking.

"Come again?" I asked her. I heard what the hell she was saying, but I wanted to know if we were talking about the same person. "Tell me all you know about that nigga," I spat at her. I could possibly have Kadeem now and forever.

After giving me a break down on the nigga, I dismissed her ass. I didn't need her for shit else. Locking the door, I had to come up with a plan to make Kadeem fall for my ass like I fell for her. She was gonna have to come to the car wash sooner or later, and this time, I wasn't letting her ass go. In the meantime, I called my assistant and told her to send Kadeem some flowers. I knew I was pushing my luck, but I had to have her. Deep in thought, my phone rung, and it was Hakeem.

"Yo," I answered.

"Nigga, let's go to the club and see some big booty bitches!" he hollered in the phone. I could tell that his ass was already fucked up. Why the hell not? I didn't have shit else to do.

"Give me a minute to put on some clothes, and I'll slide through," I mentioned to him, hanging up the phone. That nigga knew how to get me out the mood I was in.

An hour later, we were pulling up to Sweetest Pu$$y. This club had some of the baddest strippers that didn't mind doing something strange for a little piece of change. Might as well see a little ass shaking while I wait for Kadeem to fall in my hands. The rest of the night went by good, all I could think about was my bed. I already knew this hangover was gonna be something serious. I kid you not, I'm never drinking again.

***

Kadeem

"I can't believe this nigga called me another bitch's name. Who the fuck is Sherry?" I asked no one in particular as I paced the floor.

"Deem, calm down, you might be blowing this out of proportion," Shay told me as I shot daggers at her ass.

"Calm down! Would you be able to calm down if your nigga called you another bitch? My point exactly, don't tell me to calm down. I can't believe that I was this damn stupid. Damn, I feel so dumb," I told her, flopping down on the chair.

This nigga had messed my whole mood up for today.

"What you gon' do?" Shay asked me.

"I'ma sit my ass right here, and when his ass comes home, it's on. I'ma make that nigga call Shery right in front of me. Damn, I can't believe I was so fucking stupid," I confessed to Shay, letting my head hit the back of the couch. After four years, this nigga just now wanna show his true colors.

Ding-dong! The doorbell rung, breaking me out my thoughts. "Get the door for me, please," I asked Shay. I wasn't in the mood to be bothered with anybody.

"Damn bitch, you got a whole secret admirer," she told me, sitting the flowers on the table. That kinda cheered me up because I knew they were from Ahkeem. I just couldn't shake his ass.

Damn, you changed your number on a nigga. That's how we doin' it now? I hope these flowers brighten up your day, pretty lady. 454-453-6743, don't forget it. Call me; I can't wait to hear your voice. Love, Ahkeem.

"Damn bitch, he ain't givin' up, is he? You must have gold-laced pussy." She giggled.

"Bitch, I might! Naw, on the real though, I just know how to put it on his ass. You better get you a Ahkeem," I told her, smelling the roses. I didn't know how he knew, but roses were my favorite.

Me: Thank you for the flowers. They are beautiful.

Ahkeem: No problem, I can see you smiling right now. Go out with me tomorrow; I promise I'll make it worth your while.

Without hesitation, I told him yeah. Fuck Tyrese, his ass didn't deserve me. Low-down, cheating ass nigga. My spirits were crushed when his ass came walking through the door.

"Sup Shay, hey bae." He tried to kiss me, and I curved his ass.

"Don't come in here on some hey bae shit. Who the fuck is Sherry, and please don't lie?" I asked with my hands on my hips.

"What you mean, who's Sherry? I don't know no fucking Sherry," he lied. I knew he was lying because he had sweat beads forming across his forehead.

"So, since you wanna lie, you can get your shit and leave. We have nothing else to talk about," I explained to him calmly. The bitch inside me wanted to fuck his ass up, but I was better than that.

"Who the fuck you tellin' to get out? This my shit, if anything, you can get the fuck out with all the false assuming and shit. I swear your ass ain't never happy." He tried to make me feel bad, that's when I pulled out my phone.

"Ty, so this ain't your number? Gone somewhere with that bullshit. You know what, I'll get my shit and leave. Shay, can you help me pack please?" I asked her calmly.

"So, you just gon' leave and not talk it out? Fuck it then; we weren't meant to be. If your ass must know, Sherry is my damn cousin," he spat, and I turned around.

"Yo' cousin? Try again, nigga. Did you not know that I met your whole family, and I have never heard of her? Is that all you could come up with? I put up with a lot of shit, but I'm not gonna put up with this shit. I love you, Ty, but I love me more," I confessed as the tears fell. This shit was hard, and I'd never dealt with heartbreak like this.

"I'm sorry, baby; I swear that I haven't been cheating on you. Sherry was a bitch that I met before you. Nothing more, nothing less." Ty tried to touch me, but I yanked away.

"Don't fucking touch me. You want me out, so that's what the fuck I'm gon' do. Now back the fuck away from me," I informed him as I started gathering my things.

All I wanted to do right now was cry my eyes out, but I wouldn't give this nigga the satisfaction. As me and Shay were packing my things, Ty was trying to talk to me, but it all fell on deaf ears. I didn't have shit to say him right now. Maybe once things calmed down, but right now, it was still sensitive. Once I was done, I left out the house and left the key on the counter. Ty looked at me with sad eyes, but I didn't give a damn. He carried on like he didn't have a wife at home. I was going on twenty-nine, and I wanted kids. Do you know that this nigga told me that we were in a place right now to have kids? Where the fuck they do that at?

"Best friend, it's gonna be ok. Just know that you can stay with me as long as you need. You can stay with me forever if you want," she declared to me once we got in the car. I was thankful for Shay.

"Thank you, girl. I just can't believe his ass would do me like this after all we done been through, now it's fuck me," I told her, and she nodded.

"When things calm down, maybe y'all can go to counseling. You and Ty have history, no matter what y'all go through. I mean, maybe y'all can go to see where y'all went wrong. I'm not telling you to forgive him, but I can see that you love him," Shay told me as we were driving away. She was right, but I'll be damned if I be a fool for him. I knew that I was wrong, but Ahkeem was heavy on my mind. I don't know if it was the sex or if it was how caring he was.

"Shay, would I be wrong if I talked to Keem while Ty and I are on a break? I mean, only if we're talking as friends? That's all I need now anyway."

"I'm not gonna tell you what to do because you're grown, but I wouldn't open up that can of worms until you see how things are gonna work out with y'all," she told me, keeping her eyes on the road. I mean, she did have a point, but I needed someone right now. It might be wrong, but it was until Ty straightened up and realized what he has.

Chapter 6

Ahkeem

"Julie, how is business today?" I asked as soon as I walked into the shop.

"Not too bad for a Saturday. We're not that busy, but we are steady. The flowers were delivered, and I'm sure she loves them," she informed me, and I nodded. I mean, damn, she could have at least texted and said she got the bitches. I ain't gon' sweat it though; I know she will come around.

"Thank you for calling Keem's Carwash. My name is Julie, how can I help you? Yes, he's here, give me just a minute, and I'll transfer you to his office," she told whoever was on the phone. "Keem, it's Kadeem," she *told* me, and I nodded.

"Thanks, Julie, put her through," I told her, making my way to my office.

"Damn, I thought you wasn't fuckin' with a nigga no more. I'm glad you called though. What's up?"

"Keem, he was cheating on me the whole time. I just can't believe I was so stupid." She sniffled.

"Baby girl, it ain't your fault, his ass didn't deserve you anyways. Let me come where you are, or you can come to my place?" I asked her, hoping she told me yes.

"I'll meet you at your place, give me about an hour," she told me, and that was music to my ears.

"Bet, I'll see you in an hour," I told her, hanging up the phone.

Finishing the little paperwork I had, I rushed home to get ready for Kadeem. Closing down the computer, I told Julie I was gone for today. Getting in the car, I rushed to the house. When I made it there, Kadeem was sitting on my porch. Exiting the car, I made my way over to her and pulled her in a hug. From the looks of things, she needed that hug.

"What's goin' on, ma? Why it look like you've been crying?" I asked her as the tears streamed down her face.

"He cheated on me, Keem, *me.*" She pulled away and pointed to herself. *Damn,* I thought to myself.

"Come on inside, and we can talk about it. Can I get you something to drink?" I asked her, letting her inside.

"I'll take some Jack Daniels on the rocks, if you have it. If not, I'll take a Sprite," she told me, and I nodded.

"I got Jack Daniels. Oh, you tryna get drunk-drunk?" I asked her, and she giggled. That was all I was trying to do was make her smile.

After getting our drinks, we moved into the living room and chilled. I loved being around Kadeem, but I wanted more of her. I didn't want her to give me her all in one day and go back to her dude the next. I didn't want to make things complicated, but I wanted Kadeem.

"Tell me how you feel about the whole situation?" I asked, just seeing where her mind was.

"I mean, I ain't gon' lie, this shit hurts like hell. After all I did for his ass, and he did me dirty? I kinda knew that something was going on, but I couldn't place my finger on it. God, I feel so stupid."

"But how you knew he was cheating on you?" I asked, and she pulled out her phone.

"Basically, I was trying to do the right thing and break things off with you. I won't lie, the sex was incredible, but it still didn't change the fact that I'm married. Long story short, I changed my number and texted him. He ended up calling me Sherry." She broke everything down to me. Damn, would you look at God!

"Damn, that's fucked up. I won't lie though, I'm glad he fucked up. Not tryna get in y'all business, but what's your husband name?" I asked, and she looked at me like I had grown two heads.

"Tyrese, but I don't wanna talk about him right now. Can you make me feel good?" she asked me above a whisper. If that's what she wanted, I was finna do just that.

Slowly kissing her, I helped her out of her shirt and bra. Her perky breasts stood at attention, and I slowly sucked on the left one. Her head fell back, and a soft moan left her lips. That made my soldier stand to attention, but it wasn't about me; it was all about her. Popping the left breast out my mouth, I did the same to her right as her fingers massaged my scalp.

"Can I taste you?" I asked, and to my surprise, she nodded. I wasted no time stripping her out of her legging.

Now I was face to face with her bald pussy, and it was spitting at me. I wasted no time diving in face first. Slowly latching on to her pussy, I took my time pleasing her. Slurping, sucking, and nibbling on her pussy, she let out a moan.

"Ooouu Keem, eat this pussy, baby," she cooed to me, fucking my face. I did just that. "I'm cumming!" she screamed as she soaked up my face. She tried to push my head away, but I was latched on like my life depended on it.

After sucking her dry, I got up and wiped my beard off with my hand. My dick was harder than a bitch, but it wasn't about me right now, it was all about her.

"I wanna feel you," she expressed to me.

"You sure? I don't want you running off like the last time," I told her, and she nodded.

"Please, I need to feel you," she begged.

Releasing my dick, I grabbed a condom and slid it on my dick. The look in her eyes told me that she was ready for the dick. Lining my dick to her open, I slowly pushed deep inside her walls. No lie, her shit was wetter than a motherfucker. Giving her deep yet long strokes, she was moaning my name. Had me ready to bust. I slowly snatched my dick out and laid on the couch.

"Come ride this dick, ma," I told her, and she slowly climbed on my dick.

After adjusting to my size, she started riding my dick like it was going out of style.

"Ouuu shit, Keem, I'm about to cum!" she screamed as her body started to jerk.

"Keem, where you at?" my brother barged into the house. "My bad, folk, I didn't know you had company," he told me, leaving back out as fast as he came in.

"I'm sorry, Keem, I have to go." Kadeem put on her clothes and headed out the door.

Fuck, Hakeem knew how to fuck up a perfect fuck!

***

Kadeem

"Girl, what the fuck are you doing?" I asked myself looking in the mirror of my car.

It was just something about Ahkeem's ass that had me running back to him. I'm not gonna lie, that was some of the best dick I had in a long time. My husband was good, but he didn't hit spots that Ahkeem hit. It was like his dick was made just for me.

"Yes," I answered my phone, breaking me out my thoughts.

"Kadeem, where the hell are you?" Shay asked.

"I'm on the way back," I told her, and she sucked her teeth.

"You're at Ahkeem's place, aren't you?" she asked.

"Yes, I needed to feel him once again, and his brother walked in on us fucking. Shay, what is wrong with me, why can't I shake Ahkeem?"

"You're hurting, Kadeem, and you're using him to hide the hurt. I told you once, and I'll tell you again, you're playing with fire, and someone is gonna get hurt in the situation. Let things die down," she told me, and I nodded like she could see me.

"You're right; I'll see in a little bit," I told her before she ended the call.

I wanted to end things, but Ahkeem made me feel wanted, he made me feel alive again. Ahkeem was the whole package so far. When I made it to the house, Shay was sitting on the porch. It was a beautiful day out, why not? Slowly exiting my car, I made it to where she was sitting.

"Look, I told you once before that I wouldn't get in you and Ty's relationship, but he can't keep popping up over here like that. Then, I have to think of a lie because you're not here, not that I mind because you're my best friend. Either y'all gon' be together or not, but you can't play both sides," she told me, and she was right. I needed to figure this out. As long as I kept sleeping with Ahkeem, it was never gonna work with Ty, and I made that vow in front of God.

"I hear you; I need to go in and shower. I'ma turn my phone off because I don't wanna be bothered with either of them. If Ty come back by, I'll handle him. Thank you for being there for me when I feel like life isn't worth living," I told Shay, and she nodded.

"No thanks needed, that's what I'm here for. Are you gonna be ok here alone tonight? I got a date with Hakeem." She blushed. They were cute together; I can't even lie.

"I'll be fine, go out and enjoy yourself. If I'm sleep when you get back, wake me up because I wanna hear all the juicy details," I told her, and we laughed together.

Heading in the house, my phone was going off like crazy. I knew it was either Ty or Ahkeem, and I didn't wanna talk to either of them right now. I was in love with Ty, but I was also falling for Ahkeem. Lust was supposed to be fun, but my ass was catching feelings. I had to back off and get my life together.

Chapter 7

Tyrese

"Got damn, this is the hundredth time I called yo' ass, to only get the voicemail. Deem, I need you, please call me back, baby." I left her another message.

I was going crazy without Kadeem. I never understood the saying "You don't miss what you got until it's gone" until now. My ass hadn't been to work in a week, but I knew the company was left in good hands. I had to figure out a way to get my baby back.

As I was deep in thought, my phone rung, and it was Sherry's ass. She was the one that had me in this situation. *"What, Sherry? Damn, a nigga can't shit without your ass. What the fuck you want?"* I snapped.

"Damn, you don't sound happy to hear from me. I was calling to see if I can get some dick," she told me boldly. I took the phone away from my ear and looked at it. Sherry's ass had gotten bold, and her ass knew better not to call me talking that shit.

"Sherry, when I want some pussy, I'll call your ass. Until then, don't hit my line." I told her, ending the call.

I had to come up with a way to get Kadeem back. I knew that once she found out about Angel, she was gonna leave my ass for good. I had to get back good in her presence because a nigga was starving without her ass.

Dragging myself off the couch, I strolled in the kitchen to see what I could throw together. My ass couldn't cook for shit; I usually left that up to Kadeem. Opening the refrigerator, I saw all this damn food and couldn't cook shit.

Then I saw a protein shake. I grabbed it and chugged it. It would do for now. Grabbing my phone, I dialed Kadeem one last time.

"Yes, Tyrese?" she answered, using my government name. She never called me that unless she was mad, but her ass needed to get over it. I needed her ass home like yesterday.

"Baby, I'm sorry. What do I have to do to convince you to come back home? A nigga miserable without you. I know I fucked up, but I'm not perfect, and you should know that right now," I told her, and I heard her sniffle. I felt like shit because I vowed to be there when she needed me, and I couldn't do that.

"Ty, you hurt me, and I need time to heal," she started, and I cut her off.

"Baby, come home, and we can heal together. I promise I won't do anything else to hurt you."

"Give me some time, and when I'm ready, I'll come home. You know if the shoe were on the other foot, it wouldn't be like this. I love you, Ty, but I love me more," she told me before ending the call. That shit that she said pissed me off. Hell, we vowed till death do us part, and I was sticking to that. Getting comfortable on the couch, I drifted off to sleep. I didn't know how tired I was until my head hit the pillow.

I woke up from a dream that felt so real. Kadeem had the divorce papers sent here, and I was forced to sign them. The shit scared me so bad that my clothes were drenched in sweat. Shaking the feeling, I got up to take a piss. After washing my hands, I rushed back in the living room where my phone was buzzing off the hook.

"Yeah Angelica, is Angel straight?" I asked in a panicked tone.

"*She's fine, but I wanted you to know, you're gonna be a daddy again,*" she told me, and my head started pounding.

"*Come again?*" I asked hearing her loud and clear.

"*I'm pregnant, and you don't have to sound so happy. You knew what you were doing when you came in me.*"

Kadeem wanted kids, but I always told her that the time wasn't right, and here goes my side chick having my second child. This shit was mind-blowing, and Kadeem was surely divorcing my ass once shit came to the light.

"*I mean, say something, don't get quiet now,*" she told me, bumping her gums.

"*How did this happen?*" I asked dumbly.

"*Nigga, you know how it happened. You put your pole in my pond. That's what happens when you go fishing without protection.*"

"*Angelica, gone somewhere with that dumb shit. My damn wife wants a baby, and I keep turning her ass down. How you think she gon' feel about this?*"

"*I don't give a damn what she thinks. You better tell her before I come break up your happy home. Please don't play with me; you know I'm real life crazy,*" she told me before she ended the call.

Like, is today fuck with Tyrese's day or some shit? I couldn't catch a break, and I knew Angelica ass wasn't playing. I needed to fix this shit, and I mean quick.

***

Angelica

"Cocoa, I don't know who the fuck he playin' with, but he got the right one. I'll be damned if I let their asses live the good life, and me and my baby are hidden. He got life all kinds of fucked up," I vented to my best friend.

Cocoa and I go way back, and I mean way back. Both of our mamas were crack heads, and we grew up in the system. When we were old enough to get out, we ran and never looked back. Times were hard, but I wouldn't change it for nothing in this world. Growing up like we did taught us a lot of shit. Hell, we had to get it how we lived. When I was nineteen, I met Tyrese's rock-head ass in the club. He looked like money, so I was bussing it wide open for his ass. He told me that he was married, but he wasn't happy. Of course, I fell for all the lying; my ass was as gullible as they came.

A couple months of fucking around, I found out I was pregnant. Ty was my meal ticket. When I first told him, he told me to get rid of it. His ass threw me the money and everything, but wasn't about to abort her. I lied and told him that I got rid of it. Nine months later, I was pushing out a beautiful baby girl, which I named Angel Marie. It was love at first sight. Ty was mad, but when he saw Angel, all that changed. Things were good for a couple months, and he moved us to New York. He said that we were too close to home. My ass was pissed. I threatened to tell his wife, and he always told me that he would fuck me up. So we been hidin' in New York, but I wanted my family together. He paid me five-thousand dollars a month in child support, and he made sure all the bills were paid, but I wanted him.

"Bitch, you know you're not pregnant. Why you lie to that man like?" Cocoa asked me, breaking me out my thoughts. She was right, but I was gonna catch his ass slipping again; his ass couldn't get enough of me.

"I already got it covered. He never wrap up with me when we fuck, so this will be easy," I told her, and she nodded.

"So, you really gon' tell his wife about y'all affair?" she asked, and I shrugged.

"I mean, if he don't get his shit together I'ma be singing like them bitches that snitched on R Kelly," I told her, and she shook her head.

"Bitch, you dumb, but that's why I fucks with you though," she told me, and I raised my glass.

While my baby was at her grandparents' house, I had a much-needed girl's night. Cocoa and I ate and drank wine until we couldn't walk straight. Our asses went through three bottles of wine. I was drunk and horny. I would rather have Ty, but Yoshi would have to do tonight.

"Bitch, I'm finna call Yoshi and have him come beat this pussy in. You can stay if you want, but if you leave, make sure you lock the bottom lock," I told her before getting up and tripping over my feet. Damn, I was shit-faced drunk.

"You hell, I'll take the guest room, and try not to be too loud. I might have to come in and join y'all," she told me, and I looked at her ass like she was crazy.

I never been with a female, but Cocoa was bad as shit. She was about five-foot-eight and light-skinned with big titties. No homo, but my best friend was bad.

"Let me call this fool and see if he down tonight. Check this out, if he comes over and you hear me screaming, join us," I told her, and she licked her lips.

"Aye Yoshi, what you doin' tonight? Yeah, I need you to come over and beat the pussy up. Ten minutes? Ok, I'll be waiting for you," I told him, ending the call.

"Damn bitch, I wanna be like you when I grow up. Just like that, and Yoshi is on his way." She snapped her fingers, and I nodded.

"Yep, just like that. Let me freshen up before he gets here," I told her, stumbling to the hall bathroom.

Once I got in the bathroom, I relieved my bladder and jumped in the shower. I made sure to give a little extra attention to Mrs. Kitty because I knew there was gonna be a lot of sucking and fucking tonight. Feeling squeaky clean, I jumped out and dried my body off. Exiting the bathroom, Cocoa came out the guest room smelling good as shit. Slapping her on the ass, the doorbell rung.

"Go in the other room. Five minutes, come in my room." I told her, and she nodded.

Once she closed the door, I swung it open, and Yoshi was standing there looking sexy as fuck. Me and Yoshi had been messing around for as long as I could remember. Hell, before Angel popped out lookin' like Ty; I knew that she was gonna be his. When I wasn't fucking Ty, I was fucking him. Don't get the shit twisted, I wasn't a hoe by a long shot, but I got needs too.

"Damn, you gon' stand there and stare at me, or you gon' let me in?" he asked, snapping me out my thoughts. I stepped to the side and let him in.

He was already stripping, so I knew what time it was. It started in the living room, and we ended up in the kitchen. Yoshi's stroke was deadly. One long stroke, and his ass had me climbing the walls. Out the corner of my eye, I saw Cocoa sneaking up.

"Come join us," I told her, and she rushed over where he was.

"Damn!" Yoshi mumbled.

"This is how this shit is finna go. I'ma lay down, and Cocoa, you're gonna eat my pussy, and Yoshi, you gon' fuck her from the back. When I cum, we will change positions. We do this my way or no way. Are we clear?" I asked.

"Crystal," they said in unison.

As I laid on the living room floor, Cocoa crawled over to me and wasted no time nibbling in my honey box. Yoshi grabbed her ass and started drilling her. The moaning she was doing against my lips was sending me into overdrive. I grabbed a fistful of her hair and started grinding in a circular motion while she was eating my pussy.

"Oowwwee shit, Cocoa. I'm finna cum!" I screamed as she snatched the soul from my body.

When I came off my high, we switched positions as promised. Yoshi was now fucking me from the back, and the feeling was everything and more. I gave Cocoa the best head she probably ever had, and I think I liked it a little too much.

"Ahh shit, I'm about to cum," Yoshi moaned, and I tried to run from his ass, but he had a death grip on me.

Yoshi knew better than this. He didn't cum in me unless I told his ass. I was beyond pissed. If he fucked my little plan up, I wasn't fucking with his ass no more. Who was I kidding? His dick was too good for that.

"Get the fuck out!" I yelled as they stood there and looked at me. I wasn't in the mood no more thanks to Yoshi. "Get the fuck out; I'll call y'all tomorrow," I told them, rushing off to my room.

Such a good night had turned bad quick. I didn't believe in the Plan B, so I had to ride this shit out. Hopefully, his ass shit a blank. Getting myself together, I laid in my bed and drifted off to sleep.

Chapter 8

Ahkeem

I was sitting here racking my brain trying to understand why Kadeem had a nigga so hooked. To tell you the truth, Kadeem was different from the women I dated. If she were any other broad, I wouldn't be chasing her ass the way I was. Then the thought of her being with her husband made me wanna make that nigga disappear.

As I was laying on the couch, my phone rung. I looked at it, and it was Sherry's ass. I wasn't even fucking with her ass like that anymore. I quickly hit the ignore button and sent her ass right to voicemail. The fact that she called back to back five times let me know that it was important.

"Yo," I asked squeezing the bridge of my nose.

"This nigga needs to pay for how he treated me. He talked to me like I was some hoe off the street. Naw, it's not that easy; he can't just dismiss me," Sherry rambled on like I gave a damn about her or that nigga.

"Sherry, do what you gotta do, just don't hit my line with that shit."

"So, there is trouble in paradise, and he tryna get back good in wifey's grace. Wifey ain't hearin' that shit though," she told me, and that was music to a nigga's ears.

"Figure that shit out. Just don't hit this line again," I told her, ending the call.

Me: *I was thinking about you. I'm sorry that my brother walked in on us. I have been going crazy without you.*

Hell, I wasn't lying. My ass couldn't sleep, shit, or eat without her ass. Then her ass was blowing me off like I was a basic nigga. That the shit that really pissed me off. If this what love felt like, my ass didn't want any parts of it.

Kadeem: I'ma try to work things out with my husband. Sorry to lead you on, you are a really great man.

That shit pissed me off. "I was a great man." Naw it ain't even goin' down like that. Call me a bitch if you want, but it was no way in hell I was about to let them be happy. She shouldn't have put that good-good on me not once but twice. A nigga was hooked after the first dose. Grabbing my phone, I dialed Hakeem and waited for him to pick up.

"Yo," he answered, sounding high as hell.

"Bruh, I need you to do me a solid. I need you to get as much info as you can on Tyrese. I don't have his last name, but I'm sure I can get that for you."

"You must really like this girl to be digging like this. I have never seen your ass this crazy about a female."

"Just dig some shit up. Shit, I got the address, Kadeem did come to the shop. Let me get on the computer, and I'll shoot that to you," I told him, ending the call.

Once I got on the computer and got her address, I texted it to Hakeem. I knew his ass was gonna have something for me shortly, I just sat back and waited. This shit was gonna be like taking candy from a baby. Kadeem would be all mine soon!!

Damn, I didn't know I had dozed off. Grabbing my phone, I saw that I had twelve missed calls from Hakeem. He found that shit quick. Wiping the sleep out my eyes, I dialed him back.

"Damn, it's about time your ass called back. Your ass must've dozed off?" he asked as soon as he answered the phone.

"Shit, my bad, bruh. What you got for me?" I asked.

"Nigga, you wouldn't believe this shit. That nigga married and got a whole family on his wife. I don't know how his ass does it, but the baby mom and daughter live in New York. Her ass bad too," he told me, and I chuckled.

"Who ain't bad to your ass? I swear every broad you see is bad. Good looking out, bruh. Send me the information over. I plan to go New York and bring her ass back with me," I told him.

"Ya' old messy ass, I gotcha though," he told me, ending the call. As soon as I hung up, Hakeem was texting me the information. I had to make sure that everything was taken care of at the shop because I was gonna be gone for at least a week. I hope that this shit didn't backfire on me because I needed Kadeem in my life.

***

Angelica

"Who is it?" I called out as I made my way to the door.

Today was Saturday, and usually, on Saturday, we sleep in. Making it to the door, I snatched it open with a mug on my face. Like the nigga at the door was sexy as fuck, but I wanted to know what the fuck he wanted.

"Can I help you?"

"Angelica, I think we can help each other. You can help me with something, and I can do the same for you," He told me, and I looked at his ass like he was crazy.

"You want Tyrese, and I want Kadeem. Husband and wife. You help me, and Tyrese will be all yours."

"And what can I help you with?" I asked with my hand on my hips, still standing at the door.

"For starters, you can go put some clothes on. Then meet me back in the living room, and we can talk business," his ass told me.

This nigga was rude as fuck, but I respected that. I wasn't used to men telling me to put on clothes to talk; I'm used to a man lusting over every curve I had. Yeah, I was stacked from my DD breasts and my ass that you can set a glass on.

After putting on some clothes, I joined the mystery man back in the living room.

"Now what can I do for you?" I asked with my hands on my hips.

"I'ma get straight to the point, I know how you can get Tyrese ass for yourself. All you gotta do is come back to Savannah with a nigga. You show up to his door, and he's all yours. The thing is, we gotta make sure that the wife is home when all this goes down," I told her, and I saw the wheels turning.

"First off, who the hell are you?" I asked with a raise of the brows.

"None of that matters. Are you in or what?" I asked her. She was doing a little too much for me.

"I'm in! My babies and I deserve so much better than this. He has hidden us for too long. Little Mrs. Wife about to know about us," she told me, and my insides were jumping for joy.

We went over the details, and then he left faster than he came. I hope this shit didn't backfire on me. I wanted Tyrese's ass in the worst way, not only for me but for our daughter. I couldn't wait till we were one big family.

After locking up, I looked up Angel and I a flight to Savannah. Ready or not, here we come!!!

Chapter 9

Ahkeem

"Let me take you out," I told Kadeem. Her ass was tryna play a nigga, but I wasn't backing off her ass.

"I don't think that's a good idea. I told you I was finna try to work it out with my husband. I like you, but I love my husband. I hope you understand," She told me, and I felt my blood boiling.

"I mean, if you wanna call it quits, then so be it. When that nigga breaks your heart, don't come crying to me," I told her, ending the call.

It saddened me to see a woman this fine running behind a fuck nigga. It's cool though, I was just gonna do me. Grabbing the piece of blunt, I lit it up to get my mind right. My ass was gone off Kadeem's ass. I couldn't eat or sleep without her. Call me a weak nigga, but once you found the one, you kinda know it. I knew that Kadeem was married, but I wasn't that nigga. I could give her ass more than what he could.

"Ahkeem, talk to me. What's goin' on with you? Since that young lady left here, you haven't been yourself. You barely eat, and look at those damn bags under your eyes," Bonney told me, and I laughed

"Bonney, I got a little situation. I have fallen in love with a married woman. Then when her and her husband are going through shit, she come straight to me. One day, she cool with us chillin', and then the next, she wants to be with her husband." I sighed.

"I'm not gonna tell you what to do, but nothing comes out of it when you're talking to a married woman. From the looks of things, I can tell your feeling are deep for her. Don't get yourself caught up in this situation because nothing good is gonna come out of it. You are gonna be lonely and heartbroken, and she will still have her husband. Take it from me, get out of this while you can. You are a fine young man, and I'm sure that any woman would be lucky enough to have you."

Everything that she told me was real. I had to leave Kadeem along until she made up her mind. No way in hell, I was about to keep being her rebound nigga.

The rest of the day, I chilled and smoke. I was determined to get my mind right. Tomorrow was a new day, and I hope that it was better than today. After showering and getting ready for bed, I laid in the bed and stared at the ceiling. Sleep was nowhere to be found. I felt my mind wandering off on Kadeem. I wondered what her ass was doing. Shaking the urge to call her, I closed my eyes and drifted off to sleep.

The next morning, I got up and handled my hygiene. I was gonna spend all day at the carwash to catch up. Kadeem's ass had a nigga messing up on money. Now it was time to get my head back in the game. While I was getting dressed, my phone rang, and I saw it was Julie. I just hope that everything was good at the shop.

"Hey, Julie what's up? Is everything good at the shop?" I asked her.

"Business is slow today for a Wednesday. I was wondering if I could get off today about two, I need to take Mama to the doctor," she told me, and I didn't see nothing wrong with it.

"I don't see anything wrong with that. How is Mama doing?" I asked her, and she sighed.

"She tried to hide it from me, but Keira told me that she had Pancreatic Cancer. As long as she takes her medicine, she's good. If I got anything to do with it, she'll never miss taking her medicine." I nodded.

"Let me finish getting ready, and I'll be there in a minute," I told her, ending the call.

After finishing getting dressed, I grabbed a bagel and headed out the door. Making it to the carwash Julia wasn't lying; it was drier than a Sahara desert. Exiting my car, I made it on the inside. It was quiet as hell in here; I don't know why Julia didn't have the music on.

"Sup Julie, why is it so damn quiet in here? Turn some music on or some shit," I told her, heading to my office.

Looking at my clock, I saw that time had crept on me fast as hell. It was already two, and I knew Julie was finna tell me that she was gone. Just as I expected, there was a knock on the door. Closing the computer down, I got up and headed to the door. Snatching it open, Julie was standing there with her hands on her hips. I don't know if I was horny or what, but Julie was looking sexy as fuck. Shaking the thoughts about bending her over, I cleared my throat.

"Alright Julie, have a good rest of your day. Tell Mama I said hello," I told her, moving around her.

"Is there anything else I need to do before I go?" she asked with lust dripping from her voice. As bad as I wanted to be inside something warm and tight, I had to decline. I had a business to run.

"Naw, you good, I got it the rest of the day. I'll see you in the morning," I told her, and she sucked her teeth. I ignored that and moved to the front.

After Julie left, I got comfortable in the front waiting for six to come. I was about to call it a night until the door dinged. I was wondering who the fuck was coming in at the last damn minute, but money was money.

"Welcome to Keem's Carwash. What can I do for you, my man?" I asked him as he looked around admiring my shop.

Yeah, I need to get the full packageh" he told me, and I nodded.

"Cool. What's the name for pickup?" I asked him.

"Tyrese Holly," he said cockily. That made my nostrils flare. This was THE Tyrese that was giving Kadeem hell. I can't believe this nigga.

"Alright, my man, we are closing in a bit, and it will be extra for my workers to stay. Are you ok with paying the extra?" I asked him, and he threw the card on the counter.

"Money ain't an issue. I have a trip to make in the morning, and my ride needs to be clean. I would've gone to the place I usually go to, but they ass messed around and closed on a nigga," he told me like I really gave a shit.

"Cool, we'll call you when it's ready," I told him.

When he left out the door, I called the guys for them to get his car done. I went outside and helped them. My nosey ass was going through all his shit; I peeped the picture that he had of Kadeem in the visor. When I looked in the glove box, I instantly got pissed. I saw the picture of the bitch that I met in New York and a little girl that looked like it could be his daughter. This nigga was really playing with fire, and that shit was gonna come back and bite him in the ass. Kadeem ain't crazy by a long shot, and I can't see how she hadn't caught on to that shit yet. I knew she was smarter than that. I took the picture and put it in the visor with Kadeem's picture. That was his family, so I just put them together.

"Ayye, your whip ready," I informed him.

"Cool, give me fifteen minutes, and I'll be on the way," he told me before ending the call. Pussy ass nigga.

After that nigga came and got his whip, I closed up for the day. I tell you one thing, today didn't owe me shit; all that was on my mind was a blunt and my bed.

***

Kadeem

"Deem, you know you can stay here as long as you want. I actually enjoyed your company," Shay told me as I hugged her.

Shay had been nothing more than amazing. She kept me encouraged, and I would spend the rest of my life thanking her.

"I know, boo, I really do appreciate you, but I think it's time to go work things out with my husband," I told her, and she nodded.

I had been staying with her for a whole month. It was gonna be nice to get home and relax. Ty and I had been talking every other day, and I felt I made him suffer enough. I bet the house was a mess, and he had picked up a couple of pounds. I hadn't talked to Ahkeem since the last time I talked to him, and I felt was only right. Ahkeem was clouding my mind. He made things hard, and I fell in love with him, but we could never be while I was married. I could tell that he was pissed, but he respected the fact that I wanted to save my marriage.

"Alright boo, I'll call you when I get home and get settled," I told Shay while pulling her in a hugged.

"Alright. Don't forget where I live; I know how you get." I laughed because I knew what she was talking about.

After getting in the car, I rushed home. Ty swore to me that he would change change. I gave him the benefit of the doubt and forgave him. Letting him know if he did that shit again, I would leave him for good. I was too good to have to put up with his bullshit. Making it to the house, I applied a little lipgloss and exited the car. Walking up to the door, I stuck the key in and twisted the knob. As I expected, the house was a mess. Liquor bottles and trash were everywhere.

I couldn't believe that he left the place like this, but I wasn't finna touch that shit. He did it, so it was only right for him to clean it up. Moving the trash off the chair, I sat down and got comfortable. Seven o'clock came, and I heard the door opening. He flipped the light on, and he looked like he saw a ghost.

"Hey, baby. How long have you been here?" he asked, looking around the house. "And why didn't you clean this place up?"

"Hey! Nice of you to join me. First off, I didn't make this mess, so there was no way in hell I was gonna clean it up. You're a grown ass man, so it makes no sense for this house to be looking like this. I'ma say this one time and one time only, so listen close. If you ever pull what you pulled before, there won't be a you and me no more. I'm grown as fuck, and I'm not getting any younger. I want a fucking child, and I want it now. You can give it to me, or I can find a random off the street to give it to me." He grabbed me by my neck, making my pussy twitch.

"Say some shit like that again, and I'll kill your ass. Fuck with me if you want to," he told me, but he wasn't running nothing but his mouth. "And clean this damn house up." He tried it.

"Nigga, you got life fucked up! I didn't mess it up, so I ain't cleanin' it up. Take that how you want," I told him, running off to the guest bedroom.

"Hey girl," I answered my ringing phone.

"Hoe, didn't I tell your ass to call me when you made it home?" Shay fussed.

"My bad girl. I got sidetracked. This damn house is a mess, and Ty expects me to clean up; he got life fucked up if he thought I was gonna touch that shit. I pushed the trash off the chair and made myself comfortable. When his ass walked in the house, he looked like he had seen a ghost. I ran things down to him if he didn't wanna give me a baby, I could find a nigga off the streets to make that shit happen. He didn't like that, of course. His ass jacked me up, and I swear I came a little," I informed her, giggling.

"Kadeem, I swear you hell. I know you didn't tell that man that." I sucked my teeth.

"Yes, I did. Ty don't run shit but his mouth. He can fuck around and give me away if he wants to. Any nigga would be lucky to have a woman like me, and I can think of one off the top of my head that would appreciate me," I told her, and the line got quiet.

"You hell, but you are so right. I'm glad you are finally understanding your worth. I'm proud of you, boo. I was just calling to make sure you good. I'm finna take a nap; I'll hit you back later on. Try not to get jacked up anymore," she told me, ending the call.

Shay knew I was good. I wasn't even worried about Ty, but I meant what I said. Just as I got comfortable in the bed, there was a knock on the door.

"What, Ty!" I hollered with my eyes closed.

"Baby, open the door. We need to talk."

I jumped up quick as hell because it sounded urgent. Snatching the door opened, I was attacked by Ty kissing all over me. Those were the kisses that I missed so much. He threw me on the bed and snatched down my leggings. He started eating my pussy like it was his last supper.

"Kadeem, I missed you so much, baby." He managed to get out as he snatched the soul out of my body.

Closing my eyes, Ahkeem popped up in my head. I tried to shake him, but I missed him something serious. Ty couldn't hold a candle to Ahkeem. Fuck, here I was comparing the two again.

"Oooh, my God, Ty, I missed you too baby," I told him as my body started jerking. My body was on fire, and I needed Ty to put that fire out.

Ty got up and licked his lips. Releasing his dick, he started stroking it as I was playing with my pussy. Not able to take it any longer, I took my fingers out and called him over. He wasted no time diving balls deep inside my pussy.

"Fuck Ty, you better fuck this pussy baby," I moaned, and he did just that.

Just as I was about to release, he snatched his dick out of me and motioned for me to get on all fours. Shit, he didn't have to tell me twice. Ass in the air, Ty licked my ass to my pussy. This was something that he never done before, but I was enjoying the feeling. After making me cum for the fourth time, he stuck his dick back inside my pussy and started pounding it.

"Baby, who pussy is this?" he asked.

"All yours, baby," I told him, and that sent him into overdrive. Next thing I knew, he was cumming deep inside my walls.

I fell on the bed on my stomach. My mind wandered to Ahkeem. Here I was thinking about his ass after a good fuck session with my husband. It wasn't good as Ahkeem, but I wouldn't tell him that. I didn't even fight the sleep; I just welcomed it. In a matter of minutes, I was out!

Chapter 10

Tyrese

After the sex session, I was madder than a motherfucker. I could tell that another nigga had been hitting something that was only for me. I know I shouldn't be mad because I had another family tucked away, but a nigga was livid. Taking a quick shower, I exited the room and left Kadeem right there. There was no way that I could lay there and hold her knowing another nigga done been all up in my pussy.

Heading to my office, I grabbed my blunt and turned the tv on. I planned on smoking myself to sleep tonight. After the fourth blunt, my phone beeped. I knew it was Angelica ass, but I want in the mood for her ass. Ignoring her, it beeped again.

Fred: Your daughter and I are taking a road trip.

Fred: First stop is Savannah, Ga.

I knew the fuck she was lying. It wasn't time for her ass to come yet; I was just getting back good with my wife. Ain't no way in hell she was finna mess this shit up. I dialed her number, and she answered on the first ring.

"Oh, that got your attention, huh? I hope you ready because I'm tired of you hiding us. I mean, we can be a family for once and all. Once your wife find out about us, she gon' leave your ass for good."

"Angelica, don't fuckin' play with me right now. When the time is right, I'll send for y'all. Play with me if you want to, and I'll cut all the money off. Then your ass will have to get a job. You don't want that, do you?" I told her, and the line got quiet. She was thinking about that shit, and I hope she did the right thing.

"You better hurry the hell up. One week, and your secret is out," she told me before ending the call.

That was something I didn't do; I didn't take orders from no damn body. I was gonna hurt her feelings if she thought she was gonna come here messing up my marriage. She better stay in her place; side chicks don't have no say so. Getting comfortable on the chair, I drifted off into a slumber.

I was woken up from a bad nightmare, drenched in sweat. I dreamed about Kadeem finding out about Angel and Angelica and leaving my ass for good. Shaking the thought, I got up and handled my hygiene. After I was done, I joined Kadeem in the kitchen.

"Good morning, husband," she spoke all bubbly.

"Morning, wifey! What your ass in here cookin'? I knew your ass was gonna clean up the house. This good dick got you cookin' and shit," I told her joking.

"Now you know good and well I can't stay in this house like this. I don't see how your ass did. I'm cooking pancakes and sausage. I probably won't be home till later tonight. I been neglecting my business, and I got a couple clients that want to meet up today," she told me, but I wasn't convinced.

"And why can't they come to the house?" I asked, and she put her hands on her hips.

"Now you know better than that. I don't know these people, ain't no way in hell I'm about to bring them here. They could be killers. I rather just meet in a public place. I'll text you the address if it makes you feel better," she told me.

"Do you, baby, I ain't mad at you," I told her, grabbing a piece of sausage. "You better not be giving my pussy away," I told her, slapping her on the ass.

The look she gave me was an uneasy look like she was hiding some shit. I walked off and put that thought in the back of my mind. I knew Kadeem's ass wasn't crazy, and I knew she valued her life.

I got myself together to head to work. When I left the house, Kadeem was on the phone with Shay. Shay was cool people, and I was glad she had a friend like her. Pulling up to the job, I got out and headed inside. Today was one of the days we went over new projects. Making it inside, Jack and Hakeem were standing by the coffee pot chopping it up.

"What's up, y'all?" I asked, dapping them up.

"Shit, same shit, just different days," Hakeem told me, and he ain't never lied.

Hakeem and I go way back, and he didn't approve of what I was doing to Kadeem. I mean, he didn't like it, but his ass didn't speak on it either. I really needed him right now. Last night was still playing in the back of my head.

"Hakeem, let me ask you something. How can you tell if your ole lady been cheatin' on you?" I came straight out with it. He gave me a confused look and shrugged.

"Let just say shawty ain't crazy. She values her life and the shit that I do for her. I can tell you one thing, I know how that pussy feels, and if she was giving it up, I could tell. Trouble in paradise, my man?" he asked.

"Naw, no trouble, my man. Just shit felt different last night when I was fucking her. All the years we done been together, ain't no shit like this happened. Had me in my feelings. I wanted to hold her ass and kill her at the same time."

"But why though? How you think she gon' feel when she find out about Angelica and Angel? That shit gon' break her," he told me, and I nodded.

"If I got anything to do with it, she will never find out about them."

"Nigga, look around you. What happens in the dark always come to light. Kadeem ain't crazy, man. I would've been left your ass when you wouldn't give me a child. Then you got a whole family in New York, that shit ain't cool. Let me get her; I'll show you how to treat her," he told me, and I attacked his ass. We were boysh but Kadeem was my bitch, and he knew that shit.

"Break that shit up. Hakeem, you were wrong, and Tyrese, you were wrong. Y'all been boys for a while, and Hakeem you was out of line for what you said." Jack stood in between us.

"I'm just saying, he asked for my opinion. I was just being real with him. Fuck all this; I'm out," Hakeem told us walking out the door. I guess I deserved that, but his ass was out of line. Like he was trying to get my woman.

The rest of the day, Hakeem's words were in the back of my mind. I couldn't even focus on the task at hand. Kadeem texted me the address where she was, and I decided to pop up on her ass.

"Jack, I'm out. Lock up when you leave," I told him, dapping him up.

Getting in the car, what Hakeem told me popped up in my head. I knew this was gonna break Kadeem's heart, and I had no intentions on doing that. That's why I kept her and Angelica miles and miles away from each other. I wanted to give her a baby, but I didn't wanna neglect Angel. She was my pride and joy.

Making it to the address, I sat in the car watching Kadeem and the nigga interact. I could tell by her body language that they knew each other. I just sat in the car and watched to make sure no shit didn't go down. After watching them for thirty minutes, I decided to get my ass home. I decided to surprise Kadeem with dinner since I hadn't been the best husband.

What was almost a great night turned into a bad one when I pulled up in driveway. Damn, I just couldn't catch a fucking break!

***

Angelica

"Didn't I tell you that you couldn't hide us forever? I get so tired of listening to you telling me that we are gonna be a family and you're still here playing house with your wife. Angel and this baby need you," I told him.

"Angelica, what the hell are you doing here? I told you that I needed time, and we were going to be together. You can't be here; my wife will be home in a minute. Take my card and go get y'all a hotel. Once I make sure my wife is good, I'll come be with y'all. Please don't make me beg," he told me, handing me the card. I snatched it and got in my car.

"Hey, Daddy. You got a nice house. Can I come in and look around?" Angel asked. How could he tell a child so cute no?

"Not today, baby girl, but very soon," he told her, and it broke my heart to see her cry. All she wanted was her daddy, and I couldn't do nothing about it.

"Angel, it's ok! We'll go get some ice cream and a room with a hot tub. We can get in and stay in it all night. How does that sound, baby?" I asked her, and she dried her eyes.

"I like that, Mommy. Will Daddy be coming too?"

"I'll be there before you go to sleep. Go ahead and go get comfortable. I'll see y'all in a minute."

We buckled up and went on about our business. I looked into my mirror, and I saw a car following us. I instantly tensed up because I was in a position before where a crazy ex was stalking me. That was some crazy shit, and I couldn't imagine it happening again. I cut a few corners, I lost whoever was following us, and I felt relieved.

"Angel, what kind of ice cream you want?" I asked my daughter, pulling up to Cold Stone.

"Strawberry with rainbow sprinkles," she told me, and I smiled. No matter how old she got, she still loved her rainbow sprinkles.

"Welcome to Cold Stone, what can I get you today?"

"Yes, I'll have a pint of strawberry ice cream with rainbow sprinkles, and a pint of strawberry cheesecake ice cream."

"Can I get you anything else?" she asked, and I pulled up the window.

"23.05," she told me, and I handed her Tyrese black card.

"Have a great night," she told me handing me the ice cream.

"Angel, do you want anything to eat before we go to the room, or do you wanna do room service?"

"Room service. I really just wanna eat my ice cream and wait for Daddy to come," she told me sadly. My baby loved her some Tyrese, and it broke me to see her like this. This was our mini vacation, and I planned to make the best of it. Before we left, I planned on breaking up a happy home. Hell, if we couldn't be happy, his ass wasn't gonna be happy either.

Making it to the hotel, I paid for us a room for a whole week. Good thing Angel was on spring break. After getting our key, I grabbed our things, and we headed up to the room. I had been in some nice rooms, but this one was the nicest hands down. We had double beds ,and mirrors were all around the room. Let's not get started on the bathroom; it had a jacuzzi, a hot tub, and a shower. I was in heaven.

"Angel, put the ice cream in the freezer and let's get comfortable. I'ma run us some water in the jacuzzi. Your daddy will be here before you know it," I told her, and her face brightened up.

After a much needed relaxing session, Angel and I put on and got in bed. Tonight was all about her. We ate our ice cream and watched movie. The sad thing about it was she wanted her father, and his ass didn't want to be bothered. We were in his city, and I didn't mind cutting up.

Me: Angel is waiting up for you. I suggest you make it here, or I'll come show my ass. Please don't play with me.

Baby daddy: I'll be there in a minute. I gotta finish up here first.

Me: 30 minutes! If you're not here by then, I'll coming to show my ass. What is wifey gonna think about your other family?

Me: I said I'm coming. If you bring your ass back over here, I promise I'll hurt your feelings. Play with me if you want to.

"Mommy, when is Daddy coming?" Angel asked, yawning. My poor baby.

"He'll be here in thirty minutes. You can take a quick nap, and I'll wake you when he gets here," I told her, kissing her on the forehead. With that, she drifted off to sleep.

Thirty minutes passed, and still no Tyrese. I didn't wanna wake my baby for her to see me act a fool. I grabbed my phone and dialed his number. It rung one time and went to voicemail. I knew he was with her when he should've been here with us. That pissed me off! I called back to back only to get the voicemail. That only angered me further. I threw my phone on the bed and drifted off to sleep. Tomorrow was a new day, and I was ready for my messiness to begin. Play me once, shame on you, play me twice, shame on me. I knew one thing, he wasn't gonna fool me again. I was claiming what was owed to me!

Chapter 11

Kadeem

"Answer the phone, Ty. The same number been callin' you for the last thirty minutes," I told him pissed.

"That's one of the workers from work, and I'll see him in the morning. Come on, let's finish dinner so that I can put some dick in your life," he told me, and I wasn't in the mood for him.

My mind drifted off to Ahkeem, that's who I wanted. I missed him more than he'd ever know. Here I was saving something that wasn't meant to be saved. Maybe it was time for me to let go and give this marriage up. I was the only one holding on anyways; I felt like Ty checked out years ago. I knew this was crazy, but I felt like he was hiding something from me. I wasn't quite sure what it was, but it felt like it was something that was gonna tear me apart. Grabbing my phone, I dialed Shay. I needed an alibi so I could go see Ahkeem. I needed him right now.

"Kadeem, everything good?" she asked as soon as I picked up the phone.

"Can you come get me? I can't stand to look at Ty's ass right now. I would drive, but I'm fucked up right now," I informed her, staring at him daring him to say something.

"Give me a minute; I'm on the way," she told me, ending the call.

"So you gon' leave and not talk about this? See, that's your damn problem, you always running away from shit, and you never wanna talk about it." I stopped dead in my tracks.

"Ty, I'm done with this shit. When you grow the hell up, call me. I know that wasn't a nigga from the job. I was born at night, but not last night," I told him, proceeding in the room to pack a bad.

He didn't follow me behind me, so l knew I was right. I couldn't believe I wasted years on someone that didn't give a damn about himself. How could I be so stupid to think that he was gonna change? After packing some clothes, I heard Shay pull up outside. I grabbed my bag and headed out the door. Ty ass was looking like his ass wanted to say something, but I wish he would the fuck would.

"Girl, everything good?" Shay asked me as soon as I got in the car.

"No, I need to see Ahkeem. Can you take me over there?" I asked her.

"Kadeem, are you serious? What happened in there?" she asked me, but I didn't want to talk about that right now. I needed Ahkeem.

"I promise we will talk about it later, but I need Ahkeem right now."

"If that's where you wanna go, I guess we can go over there. This ain't over, so please be ready to talk about this when everything is said and done," she told me, and I nodded.

On the ride over to Ahkeem's place, my mind was all over the place. Where did I go wrong, to be treated the way I was treated? I thought I was a great woman and a better wife. Evidently, I was wrong. When we made it to Ahkeem's house, I got out the car and ran to his door. It was pouring outside, but none of that mattered right now. Banging on the door, I waited for someone to answer. The porch light came on, and I heard the locks being unlocked. The door was swung open, and I fell in someone arms. It wasn't Ahkeem, so I knew it was Bonney.

"Kadeem, what's going on, baby?" she asked me.

"Is Ahkeem home? I need him right now," I told her, rushing into the house.

"Kadeem, I don't think that's a good idea. You're a married woman, and I don't want to see him get hurt," she told me, and I stopped in my tracked.

"Was a married woman. I'm done with my husband, and I want Ahkeem. He makes me happy, and I want him. I can promise you that I'm done with my husband," I told her, taking off my ring.

Making it to Keem's room, I twisted the knob and entered. He looked like he was sleeping so peacefully. I walked over to his bed and got inside. I laid my head on his bare chest. This felt so good, and I could stay like this forever. Ahkeem was someone that I could see the rest of my life with. Ahkeem had a good head on his shoulder and was a person that loved hard. I saw that in him.

"Kadeem, what are you doing here? I thought you wanted to work on your marriage? I can't do this with you; I'ma need you to go home to your husband, ma."

"I'm done with my husband; all I want is you, Ahkeem." I cried.

"Let's be for real, ma. How do I know that you're done with him? How do I know that when things aren't going good with us that you aren't gonna go to your husband? I can't do this with you until I see some divorce papers," he told me, and the tears fell. I understood that, but I needed to feel him right now. Whatever happened after this, I would just have to deal with.

"Please don't do this, Ahkeem. Make love to me please," I damn near begged. The way Ahkeem fucked me was different than the way my husband fucked me. I needed him like the air I breathed, that's how bad it was.

"Ma, I can't do that. You and your husband are going through some shit, and I don't want my heart getting hurt. Figure the shit out, and holla at me when the papers are signed," he told me, basically dismissing me. "Bonney, will show you the door." I felt like a fool. Here I was spilling my feelings, and Ahkeem didn't feel the same way about me.

I picked my feelings up off the floor and ran out his house. I was a fool for even telling him all this shit, and he still told me that he wasn't doing this with me. When I made it outside, Shay was still there waiting for me. I dragged myself to the car and got in. This was the hardest thing for me; I didn't do well with rejection.

"He doesn't love me no more." I cried, and Shay was there rubbing my back.

"Kadeem, you're hurting, you can't expect him to pick up where y'all left off. If you really done with Tyrese, get a divorce and show Ahkeem that it's really over. I just think you're hurting right now, and you and Ty need a break to think about things. I won't tell you what to do with your life, but you can't leave one man to go to another one that you used to mess with. Give yourself time to heal; things will fall in place," Shay told me, and I nodded.

With that, I went to Shay's house and cried my eyes out. This was something that I didn't want to experience.

Heartbreak was something that I never thought would happen to me. I thought Ty was gonna be my one and only, but boy was I wrong. I cried so much that I cried myself to sleep. Love was something that didn't live here no more. If it wasn't about Kadeem, I didn't give a fuck about it. Tyrese made me like this.

***

Ahkeem

I wanted to run after Kadeem, but I felt like I should fall back. I didn't wanna mess up a happy home even though I wanted Kadeem. Seeing her broken like that did something to me, but I couldn't find myself being the side nigga. I deserved more than that. If Kadeem was for real about getting a divorce, then maybe I could see where things went with us.

"Son, I'm proud of you. I can tell that you love her, but I also see that you love yourself more. If she was for real about divorce, then she will find her way back to you. I saw that she was hurting and was only saying those things because she was hurting. I've been there and done what Kadeem is doing to you. If it's meant to be, then it will be. I can tell you that there is someone out there for you; it may be Kadeem. Let her get her stuff figured out and go from there."

"Bonney, you just don't know it took everything in me not to hold her. The fact that she came over here crying did some shit to me. Never in life have I liked someone the way I like Kadeem. This shit is hard," I told Bonney. I was thankful for a woman like Bonney. She reminded me so much of my grandma.

"I know, son, and she will be back if it's God's will. You never know, he might have somebody better for you. Kadeem is going through too much, and she has too much baggage. Come on, I made you breakfast before you go to work."

Bonney had whipped me up some pancakes, sausage, hashbrowns, and eggs. I didn't want for anything as long as I had Bonney around. I thanked her and swallowed my food. Today was a busy day at the carwash, and I made sure not to miss it. Finishing off my orange juice, I grabbed my keys and headed out the door. When I made it to the carwash, we had cars lined up in the street, and that's just what I needed to see. I parked my car and headed for the door. Making it inside the shop, it was noisy as could be. That was the sound of money.

"Morning, Julia. How is the schedule looking today?"

"Sup, boss. It's pretty busy today; we're booked out to at least eight," she told me, and I nodded. Glad I didn't dress up today because I knew that I would be outside helping today.

"Good! Let me go sit my stuff down and head outside," I told her, heading to my office.

"Before you go in, I told her that you weren't here. She insisted on staying until you got here." I looked at her sideways.

"Why didn't you call me before you let her in my office? You know I don't play that shit with people being in my office when I'm not here. How long has she been here?" I asked her.

"Since we opened. I'm sorry, Ahkeem, she looked defeated," she told me, and I nodded. Walking to the office, I pushed the door open, and Kadeem jumped.

"What are you doing here?" I asked her as my nostrils flared. She just couldn't get it through her thick ass head.

"I needed to see you. I wanted to apologize about last night. I didn't mean to come over and act like I did. Then when you dismissed me, I felt defeated. Then you told me that I needed to do what I had to do first before we could ever be," she told me, twisting my words.

"Kadeem, I think you should leave. You could've text me that shit. Like I said and will still say, we don't have shit to talk about until you get a divorce."

"I can't live without you, Ahkeem. Tell me that you still care about me."

"Kadeem, I will always care about you as a person, but I refuse to be your rebound nigga. Handle that shit, and we can talk about us."

"I will not give up on us. I will show you that I'm all in with this." I chuckled.

She got up from my desk and left. This shit was mind-blowing. She didn't say anything about a divorce, so I knew her ass wasn't serious. I wasn't gonna wait for ass forever. As much as I tried to deny it, I was falling for Kadeem, and there was no stopping it. I just couldn't get over the fact that she was still giving that fuck nigga the time of the day. I wanted to tell her about what I saw in his car when I was cleaning it, but that wasn't my place. I could tell that she was never really in the car because I didn't see much of her stuff. If she were my woman, I would have all her shit in my car. To let everyone know how proud I was to have her as a woman. I mean, I could tell her about the shit that I saw, but that wasn't my place. She would have to learn the hard way.

After getting myself together, I headed outside to help detail some cars. One hit, and I was tired than a mother fucker. I left to go inside and let the worker finish the rest. I still had payroll and ordering to do. I was a nigga that didn't like to run out of shit, and I liked it where my workers got paid on time. They took care of me, and I made sure I took care of them. Kadeem popped up in my head, and I quickly shook her out. I meant what I said when I said I wasn't fucking with her until she handled her business.

"Boss, some woman is here to see you, and no, it's not Kadeem. I haven't seen her around here before." Julia barged into my office. I mugged her ass because she knew I didn't play that shit about coming in my office without knocking.

"Send her in, and don't be bussing in my shit like that. That'll get your feeling hurt real quick."

When she walked in, I remembered ole girl from New York. I just wondered what the hell she wanted. "What can I do for you?" I asked her.

"I'm ready to carry on with the plan. I will do anything to have Tyrese with us. My daughter misses her daddy, and I can't do this pregnancy along. Just help me out, and we will both get something out the deal." She told me, and she had a point.

"Ok, go back to where you were, and I'll have Tyrese followed there. The person that will be following him will tip Kadeem off that he's there. You will have Tyrese, and I can hold Kadeem," I told her, liking the way that sounded.

"Thank you, I really appreciate you, Ahkeem." I looked at her ass like she was crazy. I didn't tell her ass my name. "I did my research on you. Don't look at me like that. Let me get out of here," she told me, exiting my office.

I had a plan in process, and I hoped this shit didn't backfire on me. I knew that Hakeem worked for this nigga, and he told him all of his business. I was finna set it up where Hakeem followed him and took pictures of him getting out of his car and going into the hotel. I was gonna use my work phone to send them to her. I know this was a bitch move, but I rather for her to see how Tyrese was doing her ass. Getting myself together, I got my shit and headed out the shop with a smile on my face.

Me: I need a favor, bruh. You know I wouln't ask if I didn't need it.

Hakeem: What's up, bruh? You know I got you.

Me: Meet me at the crib, and I'll go over it.

Hakeem: Bet! On the way.

When I made it to the crib, Hakeem was pulling up to. After dapping him up, we headed into the house and got down to business. I told Bonney earlier that she could have the rest of the day off. I just didn't wanna hear her mouth about this backfiring on me.

"So, you work with Tyrese, right? The one that's married to Kadeem and the baby mother of Angelica."

"Hell yeah. That nigga almost got the business the other day. You know I don't fuck with nobody, and when you're wrong, you're wrong. I told him that things were gonna hit the fan once Kadeem found out about Angelica. This nigga told me to mind my fucking business. I told him that Kadeem needed a man like me. No offense, bruh, I know that you were fucking with her. I just told him that to piss him off."

"No offense taken. I need for you to set some shit up so that Kadeem finds out that this pussy is cheating on her. The bitch that he knocked up is here in town. She came by the shop today and asked for my help. I told her that I would do what I could. Did you know her ass was pregnant again?" I asked, and he shook his head no.

"That's a damn shame. Kadeem is gonna blow her shit. All they argue about is having a baby, and this nigga done had two on her," he told me, shaking his head.

"That's what I'm saying. Do this for me, and I gotcha little, bro," I told him, and he got up and headed for the door.

"You know I got you, bro," he told me, leaving out the door. Shit was about to hit the fan and real quick.

Chapter 12

Kadeem

"Shay, let's get dressed and go out tonight. I could use a drink and some fun," I told my best friend. All I was doing was lounging around and soaking in my sadness.

"Bitch, you ain't said nothin' but a word. Get dressed, and we can got to club One on One. I heard it was popping on Friday night." I started popping my ass. I can't remember the last time I went to the club, but I was finna definitely enjoy myself tonight.

"What you wearin' tonight?" I asked Shay as she curled her hair.

"Hell, I don't know yet. It's gonna be something sexy, and you know this." She popped her ass.

"Let's take a couple of shots before we go because you know how my nerves are. I don't want to think about Ty or Ahkeem's ass tonight. I just wanna let my hair down and have fun."

"Ooouuu bitch, you tryna show out tonight. Show the fuck out then," she told me as we started twerking in the bathroom.

There was never a dull moment with Shay; she kept me sane. Her motto was fuck and keep it moving. She wasn't looking for love, she was looking for a quick fuck, and that was it. I just don't see how she don't catch feeling for the men she fucks with. I mean, if the dick good, we're fighting if you give it to anyone else. That's how I felt about Ahkeem, but since he wasn't fucking with me right now, I had no say so.

After two shots of Tequila, I was feeling right. I was ready to get dressed and throw this ass in a circle and make Ty wished he never fucked me over. After getting dressed, Shay and I headed out the door. We decided to catch a Uber because I knew that we were gonna be too drunk to drive. I was finna take my ass in the club and party like I had just turned twenty-one. Getting in the Uber, we told him where we were going, and we were on the way.

"Bitch, why this car smell like ass?" I whispered to Shay. The alcohol had me on a whole 'nother level.

"Bitch, shut up before he kicks us out. These heels too high to be walkin'," she told me, and she ain't never lied.

When we made it to the club, we paid the driver and got out. We fixed ourselves before looping arms and heading to the club doors. We could tell the club was jumping from the outside. When we finally made it in the club, Future's *"Crushed Up"* was playing. That was my shit; I had to rap along with them.

"Half a ticket for my wrist, spill so big,

I put five pointers in the face, you can see it,

I just put my whole damn arm in the fridge,

Ten chains on, Lucky Charms, I'm the shit."

I was feeling myself as I moved my body to the beat. I felt as I was the only one in the club as I started throwing my ass in a circle. Shay was right beside me hyping me up. She was the real MVP. When the music went off, I grabbed Shay, and we headed to the bar. When we made it there, I felt my phone vibrating in my bag. I got the shock of my life when I got a picture of my husband heading inside the hotel. I knew I wasn't supposed to care, but I couldn't help it. The waterworks started.

"Bitch, what the fuck is wrong with you?" Shay asked me. I couldn't say anything at the moment, so I showed her the picture. "I know you lyin'; let's go kill that nigga," she told me as I took the shot of Henny.

When we made it outside, we flagged down a cab and got in. Shay gave him the address to her house. She had done sobered up real quick. When we made it to the house, we jumped out the cab and jumped into Shay's car. I was still a wreck, my leg was shaking, and I couldn't keep the tears from falling. There was always a feeling in the back on my mind that he was cheating, but seeing him actually going into the hotel really fucked me up. There was only one Holiday Inn by us, so that's where we headed.

"I can't believe this shit. After everything I did for his ass, it's fuck me? Naw, fuck you, Tyrese!" I screamed, not caring if people were looking at me crazy. I jumped out the car, and Shay was on my heals.

"Good evening, I'm here to set up before my husband arrives. He told me that I could come get the key from you,"

"Aww wow, that's amazing, I'm so happy for y'all. I would still need to call your husband and make sure that it's ok. What is your husband's name?" she asked me as I texted Ahkeem and told him to play along with me.

"Tyrese Holly. That's not necessary, I will call him, and he will tell you himself," I told her dialing Ahkeem's number.

"Baby, I'm at the hotel that you had reserved for us, and the lady won't give me a key until she talks to you," I told him, praying that he would do me this favor. I put the phone on speaker and waited for him to answer.

"Bae, this was supposed to be a surprise, but I guess since you're already there, you can get a key. I know you're gonna make it worth my while," he told me, and I blushed.

"I gotcha, baby," I told her, looking at the receptionist.

She got all the information she needed from him and gave me the key. This shit was too easy; it was like taking candy from a baby. After thanking her, Shay and I headed for the elevator. Nothing was said until we got in the elevator and was on our way up.

"Bitch, that was a close one. You better thank Ahkeem for doing you this favor."

"That's already in the motion. Once I see this with my own eyes, I will thank Ahkeem personally," I told her, and she looked at me sideways.

My heart was beating out of my chest. I wasn't sure what I was about to walk into. Sticking the key in the hole, my breath got caught in my throat as I saw Ty fucking the shit out of some random. I mean, he was fucking her harder than he fucked me. I took off my heels and charged at their ass. I just couldn't believe that I was seeing this shit. While I was whooping the hoe's ass, Ty went in the bathroom to put some clothes on. I looked in the bed beside them, and I saw a child, a beautiful little girl. His ass couldn't give me a child because he had a whole another family.

"That's enough, Kadeem. There is a child over there." Shay snatched me off the bitch's ass.

"Oh, you must be Kaddem. It's nice to meet you, and the pictures don't do you any justice. You are gorgeous, and I see why Ty won't leave you alone," She told me as I bucked at her ass.

"You nasty hoe, put some clothes on. I can't believe y'all was fucking with that baby right there. Who the fuck are you?" I asked as she grabbed the robe to cover up.

"I'm the one he was coming to see when he told you he had a meetings in New York. This is Angel, our daughter, and this is our new bundle of joy." She started rubbing her pudge, and I was livid.

"Shay, wait outside, and don't let no one in this bitch," I told her, and she nodded.

Just as she walked outside, Ty's ass came strolling out the bathroom like he didn't just fuck this hoe. I wanted to slap that smirk off his face. Tyrese came out the bathroom shaking his head, and I charged at his ass.

"You son of a bitch, after all I did for you, and you do me like this? I told you time after time that I wanted a baby, and you told me the same thing every time—'now is not the time," I told him, mocking his words. "You couldn't give me a baby because you were too busy playing house with your other family. I ought to fuck you up, but I'ma let you have this one."

"You might be his wife, but I'm more than you'll ever be."

"Kadeem calm the fuck down. This ain't what it looks like. Let me explain."

"Bitch, fuck you. You know what, y'all deserve each other. Don't think that you gon' keep him. He gon' do the same shit he did to me. Fuck you both and have a good life. I hope you both rot in hell!" I told them as I was heading for the door. Something hit me in the back of the head, and I blacked out.

***

Shay

I was outside beating myself up for not telling Kadeem about the incident that I saw the other night. What kind of best friend was I to be holding onto something like this? While I was standing at the door, it got quiet all of a sudden. Just as I was about to peep my head inside, the receptionist came walking with a wanna be cop.

"I was called and told that it was a lot of noise in this room. I'ma need you to move out the way," she told me with her hands on her hips.

"Ain't nothin' goin' on here. Tonight is their anniversary; I'm sure they're fine," I told her, but I could tell that she wasn't convinced.

"I'm sorry, I'ma still need to check the room. So, if you will excuse me," she told me, damn near pushing me out the way.

When she opened the door, I saw Kadeem on the floor, and my heart dropped in my chest. Ain't no tellin' how long she was there. I just hoped that she was good. They went in and tried to close the door, but I put my foot in the doorway.

"I need to make sure she's straight," I told her, matching her mug. This bitch could mess with me if she wanted to. I would have her ass floating in the river; I tried to leave that side where it was. People were always trying me.

"We're gonna have to call the police and the ambulance. Nobody move," she told us, but she had me fucked up. I was finna drag Kadeem out this bitch.

"We just had a little disagreement. Everything is cool here; she just passed out with everything that was thrown at her," Ty told her, had me looking at his ass sideways.

Looking down on the floor, I saw Kadeem was bleeding. I grabbed her and checked for a pulse. It was weak, but it was there. "We don't have time for this shit; I need to get her to the hospital. Ty, this shit is all your fault. If you would have kept your dick in your pants, none of this would have happened!" I screamed, not caring who was in the room.

"Shay, take your ass on. This is not what it looks like." I slapped the dog shit out of him. How dare he let some shit like that fly out of his mouth.

"The police are on their way," the lady told us, but I didn't give a shit.

"Tell them to meet me at the hospital; she's losing a lot of blood," I told her before throwing Kadeem over my shoulder. "Stay with me, bitch, I'm finna get you to the hospital. I can't believe that I didn't tell you about this shit when I saw it." I cried.

Throwing Kadeem in the seat, I buckled her up and headed to my side. I drove like a bat out of hell trying to get her to the hospital. The police got behind me, but I wasn't stopping until I made it to the hospital. Their asses would just have to wait until I stopped. When I pulled into the hospital, I pulled up to the Emergency room doors.

"Somebody help me. My friend is bleeding out!" I screamed as loud as I could. They rushed outside, damn near pushing me out the way.

"Can you tell us what happened?" one of the nurses asked me.

"I don't know; just please help her," I told them histerical. I just couldn't see her like that.

"We're gonna need for you to calm down; she's in good hands," one of the nurses told me, and I relaxed a little.

"I'ma need you to answer some questions for me," the short, stubby police officer told me, and I looked at his ass like he was crazy. His ass could've waited until all this shit was over.

"What you got for me?" I asked him with attitude dripping from my voice.

"Tell me what happened to your friend?" he asked, and I gave him a dumbfounded look.

"Didn't you just hear me tell her I don't know what happened to her? We went to a hotel and found her husband cheating. That is all I know," I told him truthfully. I didn't have shit to lie about.

"Ok. If you remember anything else, don't hesitate to call. I'ma let you by with the ticket because of everything going on. Have a good night," he told me, handing me one of his business cards.

I rushed inside and sat in the lobby until they got her stable. I didn't know what to do; this was all too much for me. Looking down, I saw that I had Kadeem's phone. I decided to call Ahkeem and let him know what was going on.

I needed someone here with me, and I'm sure that Kadeem would thank me when she saw him. Scrolling through her phone, I laughed because she had two Shay's in her phone. One had hearts by it, so I knew that number was mine. Going to the other one, I hit send and waited for him to pick up.

"Yo," he answered, sounding like he had just woken up. I felt like shit for waking his ass up.

"Ahkeem, it's Shay. I'm up here at the hospital with Kadeem," I started, and he cut me off.

"What the fuck did that fuck boy do to her? Is everything good?" he asked, rambling off questions. From the sound of things, he was stumbling.

"We were at the club, and Kadeem got a picture message about being at this hotel. We went over to see what that was all about. Sure enough, Ty's ass was there with some bitch that we have never seen before. Come to find out, that nigga had a whole family. Deem told me to stand outside and make sure nobody came in. The hotel security came up, and when they went inside, I saw Kadeem laying on the floor," I told him.

"What hospital y'all at?"

"St. Joseph's."

"Bet. I'm on the way," was the last I heard before the line went dead.

I sat here and waited, waited, and waited. I was getting so impatient because I didn't know what they were doing to her. Ahkeem had come in and calmed me down, telling me that Kadeem was gonna be good. I hope he was right because I didn't know what I would do if something happened to my best friend. Just as I was about to get up, I saw Tyrese walk his sorry ass in. Ahkeem's muscles in his jaw flexed and his face twisted. Oh shit, it was about to go down in this bitch.

Chapter 13

Ahkeem

"What the fuck you doin' here, bitch nigga?" I asked, walking up to Tyrese's punk ass.

"Nigga, what the fuck you mean what I'm doing here? My damn wife is here; you can get the fuck outta here with that bullshit," he told me, trying to walk past me, and I rocked his ass. The nerves of this nigga to come show his face with what he had done to Kadeem.

"Was she your wife when you cheated on her and got another bitch pregnant?" I asked him, sending blows to his face. "Was she your wife when she was home alone wondering about your ass?" I kept the punches coming.

I felt someone pull me off of him, but he deserved everything I had done to his ass. His ass better be glad I left my heat at home, or I would've probably killed his ass.

"Ahkeem, that's enough. Tyrese ain't even worth this. Go home, and I'll call you as soon as Kadeem wakes up," Shay told me, and I nodded.

"Make sure you call me, Shay, and this ain't over, pussy," I revealed to him, spitting on him.

I made my way outside the hospital and lit me a Newport. I only smoked them fuckers when I was mad. I grabbed my phone and dialed Hakeem. This nigga had to go, and I knew he was Keem's boss. Just as I was about to hang up, his ass picked.

"What's good with you, bruh?"

"*Man, this nigga got to go. He done hurt Kadeem for the last time. I tried to keep my distance from her ass until she got her mind right, but I'm not finna let this fuck boy hurt her,*" I told him, getting in my car and pulling off.

"What you got in mind? I can't stand his ass for the way he does her. I only deal with his ass because he signs my paycheck, other than that I don't fuck with him." He told me. Just what I wanted to hear.

"*I don't give a damn what happens to his ass, but I want him far away from Kadeem. When she wakes up, I'ma see where her head at. Time up for this nigga,*" I told him, and he chuckled. "*Fuck you laughin' for? I'm dead ass.*"

"*You must really like her? I never seen you act like this over a woman as long as we been alive. But I feel you though, once you find the one you know. I ain't mad at you, bro. Where you at now?*"

"*Shit pulling up to the crib, finna smoke some trees to ease my mind,*" I advised him.

"Bet! I'm finna get these last couple hours in and get my ass up and go work out," he told me as I made my way in the house.

"*Alright bro, I'ma holla at you later then,*" I revealed to him, ending the call.

I flipped on the living room light, and Bonney scared the shit out of me. Hell, by the looks of things, I scared her too.

"Bonney, why you sittin' in the dark like this? You know you have a room upstairs," I mention to her, and she nodded.

"The way you ran out scared me. I got up and came down here. Is everything ok?" she asked in a concerned tone.

"Everything cool. I got everything under control. Go on back to bed so that I can smoke my trees," I reported, and she laughed.

When she went upstairs, I took the weed box from under the cough and rolled me a couple of blunts. I had to find a way to take this nigga down without killing his ass. If I saw that nigga right now, his ass would be a goner. Lighting the blunt, I let the smoke fill my lungs. Going too far down, I started coughing.

"Ooouuu, this some good shit," I said to myself taking another pull.

When I was done, I sprayed some air freshener and walked in the kitchen to wash my hands. Getting a couple bottles of water, I headed to my room. After downing the water, I laid down on the bed with hopes of sleep finding me. That shit was impossible; I laid there looking at the ceiling wondering if Kadeem was good. Grabbing my phone, I dialed her number hoping that she would pick up.

"I was just about to call you. Kadeem is woke and alert. She kinda upset, but I bet she will be happy to see you," Shay informed me, and I smiled.

"Naw, if she wants me up there, she gon' have to tell me herself," I spoke as Kadeem's sweet voice got on the phone.

"Hey, Ahkeem. I need you right now; can you come up to the hospital?" she asked, but she had said nothing but a word. From the way she sounded, it sounded like she had been crying.

"You good, ma? I'm headed up there now," I informed her, and she sniffed.

"No, I'm not ok; just hurry up," she notified me before ended the call.

I jumped up and made my way to the house, making sure I locked up behind me. Jumping in my whip, I headed for the hospital. It took me a little over ten minutes to get there. When I made it there, I asked the lady at the desk what room Kadeem was in. After she told me, I took off to her room. Pushing the door open to her room, I heard a strong heartbeat. Was she really telling me that I was about to be a pop?

***

Kadeem

"I'ma let y'all talk, I'ma head down to the vending area. If you need me, boo, call me," Shay told us as she hugged me.

"Hey Ahkeem, I'm glad you came. First, I would like to apologize for the way that I treated you. I knew what I was doing when I led you on. Never in a million years would I have thought that I would catch my husband cheating on me. Then when I woke up, I found out that I was pregnant." She cried.

"Ssshhhh, it's alright. When I met your husband, I knew he was a fuck nigga. He doesn't deserve you, and you deserve so much better," Ahkeem stated. "One question though, is this baby mine?" he asked me, and I didn't know. I was confused when I fucked both of them.

"I don't know," I mentioned to him with my head down. I felt low and ashamed. I didn't want a baby by my no-good husband.

"Look at me, Kadeem. No matter what the outcome is, I'ma be there for you. I feel something for you that I never felt before. You are the person that I think about before I go to bed, and the same one I think of when I wake up. I knew when I met you that you was gonna hold a special part in my heart. I'm sorry the way that your husband did you, and just know if you give me a chance I'll spend the rest of my life making it up to you." Ahkeem spilled his heart to me. And I could tell that it was coming from the heart as his brown eyes pierced through my soul.

"I don't know, Keem. You are heaven sent, but I'm damaged and broken. You need someone as strong as you," I said to him and wasn't ready for what he was about to say.

"Kadeem, don't tell me what you think I need. I'm here, and you are what I want. I don't give a damn that you're pregnant, and it's a possibility that it may not be mine. Let me piece you back together. I promise you won't regret it," he told me, taking my wedding ring off. "You won't be needing this anymore," he mentioned to me, and I laughed.

"Well Kadeem, it looks like everything checked out, and you are free to go. Husband?" the nurse asked me, pointing at Ahkeem.

"Naw, boyfriend. I could never be that fuck nigga she was married to," he revealed to her, and I shook my head. Ahkeem was one hell of a man.

"Very well. Let me unhook you, and you guys are free to go. Make sure you follow up with a gynecologist."

"Oh, I'll make sure of that." Ahkeem butted in.

As promised, she unhooked me and let me go. I told Ahkeem bye and went home with Shay. I needed to get my head right with everything going on. First thing in the morning, I was heading to the courthouse to file for a divorce.

"So, you just gon' sit here and act like the chemistry between Keem and you ain't there?" Shay asked me breaking the silence.

"I'm not saying anything. I got a lot of shit to think about. First and foremost, is this baby I'm carrying inside me. I don't know who's the daddy. I feel disgusted for sleeping with both of them on the same night. I won't lie though, I enjoyed Keem more than my husband. It's like his dick was made for me. Even if this baby isn't his, we're gonna work on things. Keem is caring and loving. As for my husband, he can kiss my ass. I'm done with his ass. If this child is his, I'm putting his ass on child support. He can take care of the baby like he was doing his other family." I ranted with Shay.

"I know what you mean, boo. I'm sorry that all this happened to you. Don't worry, you can stay with me forever," She mentioned to me, sounding sincere.

"Shay, I appreciate you, girl, but I won't be staying with you forever. I need to get myself together for this baby," I informed her, rubbing my belly.

"Girl, what I done told you about thanking me? You are my best friend, and I'll do anything for you. You been ridin' for me, and I'ma ride for you. Enough with all this mushy shit. Do you want anything to eat before we head to the house?" she asked me, and my stomach growled loud as shit.

"I want a cheesesteak and some chill cheese fries. Hell, let's go to Betty Bombers, you know her cheesesteak be bomb," I told her, and she nodded.

While we were driving to the restaurant, my phone rang, and I rolled my eyes. This nigga had some nerves calling me. I had nothing to say to him because all the shit he did wasn't called for, but I'm so glad that it came to light. After declining his call, he called right back. I was annoyed with his ass right now.

"You don't have to answer that, Kadeem. His ass messed up, not the other way around. Fuck his ass," Shay told me.

"I know, but I just wanna know why he did it," I told her, answering the phone.

"Hello."

"Kadeem, let me explain. I'm sorry for what I did, and I didn't know how to tell you because I knew that you wanted a baby. I'm sorry that I failed you as a husband, but I'm hoping we could be friends," Ty told me, and I took the phone from my ear. Did this nigga say he wanted to be friends? Where the fuck they do that at?

"Tyrese, how the hell you sound, being friends? Do you really think that's gonna work? I gave you all of me while you was giving her all of you. How the hell you think that makes me feel? Like shit, huh, yeah, you right. I took all your late nights and business trips, not knowing that you had a whole family on me. So, thank you, Ty, for opening my eyes and making me see everything clearly. Fuck you, and I hope you have a happy life," I told him, hanging up the phone. I didn't know I was crying until Shay was wiping my tears.

"Get it out, baby. I know you hurtin', but you got to get it all out before you move on. I won't say it's easy because I don't know what heartbreak feels like. You know my motto, I don't get my feelings into it. You live, and you learn, let him have that, and you move the hell on," She told me as I dried my face. She was right; I needed to get Ty out of my system before I moved on with anybody.

"Thank you, Shay. I really needed that. I don't even want food anymore; I just wanna go lay down," I told her as she pulled away from Betty's.

When I made it to Shay's place, I went in my room and cried myself to sleep. Nobody told me that heartbreak would feel like this.

Chapter 14

Tyrese

I never meant to hurt my wife the way I did. Her and Angelica were never supposed to meet, and I made sure to have her hid. I don't know why Angelica came here and showed her ass like she did, and whoever tipped Kadeem off was gonna hear from me. That nigga from the hospital was gonna get dealt with too; I don't know why the fuck he thought it was ok to talk to my wife. Nigga done bumped his damn head.

"Daddy, I'm hungry. Can we go to Burger King and get something to eat?" Angel asked me, breaking me out of my thoughts.

"Hang on, baby girl. We can go do that, but first, daddy got some business to handle. After that, I'm all yours. Deal?" I asked her, and she gave me a quick nod.

Angelica was lying across the bed so-called sleep. I wasn't fucking with her like that right now. I was only here for Angel. All of this shit was her fault. If she would have just listened, none of this would have went down, but because she couldn't hold her horses, she got a nigga caught up.

"Angelica, get up. I need to run out for a minute. When I come back, I'll take Angel to get something to eat."

"What about me?" she asked, and I looked at her ass like she was crazy.

"What about you? I said what I had to say; I'll be back." I walked out the door.

As I made my way out to the car, I thought about Kadeem. I missed her something serious, but I knew that she wasn't fucking with me right now, and I wouldn't fuck with me either. Making it to the job, I made my way in and got to work. I needed to catch up on the paperwork and get everything in order for payroll. Turning on the computer, I got to work. In the middle of doing payroll, there was a knock at the door.

"Come in," I called out.

"Aye, what's going on, man?" Hakeem asked.

"Shit ain't lookin' good on the home front. I think I fucked up, man," I told him, running my hands down my face.

"Didn't I tell you that shit was gon' come back and bite you in the ass? I told you that nothing good was gonna come out of that. Now, didn't I tell you that Kadeem wasn't crazy, she peeped that shit?" I nodded.

"You did tell me that shit, and I wish I would have listened. Now Kadeem don't want shit to do with me."

"Man, she hurtin' right now. Give her some time to take all this in. If it's meant to be, she will come back. I been telling your ass all along that everything that glitters ain't gold. How do you think Kadeem felt when she walked into that room on y'all." He asked, and I looked at his ass like he was crazy. How the fuck he knew that she caught us in the hotel.

"Nigga how did you know that she caught us in the hotel. I didn't tell your ass that. Please tell me that you don't have shit to do with this. Me and you been rocking since grade school, and you did me like that." I told him standing up, pissed the fuck off.

"Man I didn't say that shit. I think you hearing shit." He told me nervous as fuck, but I knew what I hear.

"I know what the fuck I hear. Let me find out that your ass can't keep your mouth shut. You know what get the fuck out of my office." I told him dismissing his ass. "Don't worry about bringing your ass back either; you're fired," I told him.

"Nigga fuck you, and this company. I'm glad that Kadeem came to her senses." He told me exiting my office.

I can't believe this nigga though. After all, we went through; Hakeem knew all my secrets. If he wanted to out me, I think he would have done it before now. I was gonna wait to it cooled down and talk to him. Finishing up my day, I turned my computer off and exited my office. Jack had left for the day, so I locked up and headed back to the hotel. As soon as I got there, I kicked off my shoes and got comfortable. I knew that Angel was gonna start, so I got prepared. Not even 10 minutes later, Angel started/

"Daddy I changed my mind. Can we do pizza? I know you are tired so we don't have to go out. We can have it delivered here." She told me, and I nodded.

"Cool Angelica order Angel some pizza. You ain't doing nothing else with your life." I told her. I tried to restrain from cursing around Angel.

"Tyree, I don't know what is wrong with you, but you gonna stop talking to me like you ain't got no sense. You might have talked to your wife like that, but it ain't gonna fly with me." She sashed.

I decided to let that fly; I was gonna get in her ass once Angel was asleep. Now wasn't the time, I had a lot of shit on my mind. I was still caught up on how the hell Hakeem knew about the shit. I didn't take him to be a snake, but you never knew about people these days. While we waited for the pizza, I took a shower and got comfortable with Angel. I never meant to act funny around Angel, and I never wanted her to be a secret. I just wanted to have my cake and eat it too, but look where that got me. In the middle of the movie, there was a knock at the door. Angelica looked at me like she was scared to answer the door.

"Get the door and stop looking at me like that!" I boomed not meaning too.

"You know Tyrese if this is how you gonna act me and Angel can go back home. I wished I never got involved with your ass." She snapped back.

"Watch your mouth Angelica," I told her giving her that look. She knew better than to play with me.

After paying for the pizza, we sat down like one big family and ate in silence. I was missing my wife, well probably not my wife anymore. I know I should've done right by her, but sometimes shit doesn't play out like it supposed to. While eating, my phone rung. I had high hopes that it was Kadeem calling telling me that she forgave me and that I could come home. That quickly went out the window when I saw my mother name flash across the screen.

"Tyrese Holly, what the fuck is wrong with you? I didn't raise you to act like that. Your wife called me and told me that she found out about your little affair. Didn't I tell your ass to tell her about that girl and baby?" she fussed. Even I felt like shit; I felt worst now hearing it come from my mother.

"I know mama. I know I fucked up, you don't have to call me and remind me. I made this bed, and I got to fix it." I told her walking outside. I didn't want Angelica all in my business.

"I don't know if this is fixable. Kadeem sound hurt. After all, she did for your ass, and you gave her your ass to kiss. Your ass gotta be the dumbest person I know."

"Ma, I already feel like shit, you don't have to call and make me feel badder than I already feel. I will fix this; I promise." I said to her.

"You better! How is my granddaughter doing?" she asked me.

"She doing good mama. I'ma bring her around to see you tomorrow."

"OK. Well son, I'ma gets off this phone. You know I love you." She told me ending the call.

I walked back in the room and Angel was knocked out. Angelica was sitting up in the bed looking crazy. I knew she was finna start her shit, just by the way she was looking.

"Ty, what is next for us? I'm tired of having to wonder about us. If you don't want to be with me, I'll understand. Angel and I will pack up and go back home. I knew this was a bad idea." She told me.

"Angelica let me figure everything. If it's meant to be, it will be. Don't force this or this won't work." I told her straight up. She was always nagging and not giving me time to think.

"Do what you gotta do, but Angel and I won't be here forever." She told me going into the bathroom and slamming the door.

That's when I got my keys and got the hell out of dodge. I needed to take a ride to clear my mind. It might would do me good if I stayed away from Angelica for a while. Seeing that she had gotten me in this mess, I thought it was the best idea. When I made it to my house, I entered and laid down on the couch. It was lonely here without Kadeem, and my mother was right. Kadeem was the best thing to happen to me, and I gave her my ass to kiss. Deciding to give her a call, the phone went straight to voicemail. That shit did something to me, knowing that my wife had blocked me. But I guess I deserved that. After not being able to get her, I turned my phone off and drifted off to sleep. Call me selfish, but I was nothing without Kadeem. I knew that I had a child, but I wasn't even worried about her right now.

Kadeem

I was finally getting my life back on track. I had filed for a divorce, and I couldn't be happier. Things were starting to look up for me. I would have been foolish to take Tyrese back after all the hell he put me through. Once a cheater always a cheater. I had gotten my number changed and haven't spoken to him since the day it happened. Life was starting to look up for me. My main focus was on my travel business, which was bringing me in an hefty income. Shay told me that I didn't have to leave, but I felt that it was time now. I was looking at homes in country part of Savannah; I was in need of a change of scenery.

"Girl, what you in here doing?" Shay walked in scaring me.

"Don't be rolling up on me like that. If you must know, I am filling out applications for me an apartment. Before you start with, I can stay with you mess. I want something I can call my own." I told her truthfully.

"I know boo, but tell me how you're really feeling?" She asked me. I was dreading this conversation.

"I mean I guess I'm as well as expected. It's not a day that goes by that I don't think about the shit. Hell, my ass done even had nightmares about the shit." I told her.

"I know it's hard, but you are the strongest woman that I know. The way that you go around with you head high is some shit I don't think I could do. My ass would have probably killed him and her because that was straight disrespectful on both of their parts. Why would you take some vows and not stick to them?"

"Shay it's good girl. I have come to realization that I was too good for him. The way I was catering to him, and he didn't appreciate it. I have forgave them, but that shit I can't forget. I'm at peace with it all, God has somebody for me and I'ma wait for him." I told her closing the computer, and hopping up from the bed.

"I hear you, but where you going?" she asked looking crazy.

"Did you forget I had a doctor's appointment today? Ahkeem is meeting me up there. He has been there for me, even when I pushed him away." I told her blushing not even meaning too.

"Are you blushing Kadeem? Ahkeem got you doing that, so he good in my book. Just be careful with his ass too. Tell him I will fuck him up if he fucks you over." She told me, and I waved her off.

"Ahkeem is the good guy. He swear that he knows this is his baby, but I dunno though because I slept with both of them that day. I should feel bad about it, but I don't." I told her shrugging.

"Alright boo. I'm finna get out of here; I'll talk to you when I get home." She told me hugging me.

I finished getting ready and made my way to the doctors office. Making it there, I didn't see Ahkeem's car. That just let me know that he hadn't made it there yet. Stepping out the car, I made my way inside and checked in. After starting on the paperwork, I spotted Ahkeem walking in. His ass looked good enough to eat.

"I thought that you was gonna stand me up," I told him pulling him in for a hug.

"I would never stand you u; just something came up that I needed to handle. I wouldn't miss this for nothing in the world. What kind of man would I be to let you do this alone?" he asked breaking the hug.

"Kadeem Holly," the nurse called me to the back. Ahkeem grabbed my hand, and we walked back like one of the happiest couples.

When we made it back, the nurse got my vital and urine. Once I was done, she sat me in the room, and we waited for the doctor to come in. Glancing over at Ahkeem, he looked nervous as hell. I couldn't do nothing but laugh.

"Keem, what you over there thinking about? You are looking all nervous and shit." I mentioned to him, and he chuckled.

"Ain't nobody looking nervous. I'm just thinking about how life will be once the baby gets here. Like I told you before this is my baby, I don't care if the DNA test come back and it's not mined. I don't want you fooling with your ex-husband no more." He informed me walking over to where I was.

"You don't have to worry about that. Hell, I didn't even let him know I was pregnant. Somehow, I feel like this baby is yours." I told him, and he stared at me.

Good afternoon, mom and dad. My name is Dr. Reece, and I will be with you through these nine months. I have it confirmed that you are indeed pregnant. I would like to set up and ultrasound to figure out how many weeks you are. Today's appointment is to get to know you and answer any questions that you may have." A tall, dark-skinned woman told us.

"Is it possible to get a DNA test on the baby while she is pregnant, or do we have to wait?" Ahkeem asked, and I knew this was coming.

"Yes, that is possible after eight weeks. We can do a blood test on mom and swab your cheek. It won't hurt the baby, and it will give you a peace of mind. Is this something that you guys wanna do?" She asked looking back and forth from Ahkeem and I.

"I mean it don't matter, but if that's what he wanna do, yes we can do it," I snapped on her, not meaning to.

"Very well. We can get that set up once we figure out how far along you are." She told us, and I was ready to go. What turned out to be a good day, turned back quick. "Any other questions for me?"She asked, and I nodded no. "Well, it was good to meet you guys. I will see you back on the your next appointment, and you all have a good day." She told us walking out the room.

We got up and made our way to the front to check out. The receptionist made my next appointment, and I headed outside. Ahkeem was talking to me, but I was trying to block him out. For someone that didn't care if the baby was his or not, was surely asking a lot of questions.

"Kadeem hold up." He asked me, and I stopped dead in my tracks.

"What Ahkeem!" I hollered not meaning too.

"What wrong Kadeem? How can you get mad at me for wanting to know if this baby is mine or not? Like I will told you and will still say, I don't care if it's mines or not I'ma take care of it." He told me, and I rolled my eyes

"Ok." Was all I said before I headed outside.

"Kadeem did I say anything wrong? I just want to know, but it doesn't matter."

"If it doesn't matter, why are you going out your way to ask about it?" I asked stopping dead in my tracks.

"Kadeem I'm sorry baby, forgive me. I never meant to make you feel anyway. Come on let me take you to lunch." He told me, but I wanted to be alone. "Kadeem so just because I wanna know if the baby mine, you mad. I told you that I got y'all no matter what and that ain't changing. I could care less if it's mine, but you have to understand where I'm coming from. If the shoe was on the other foot, you wanna know right?" he asked me, but I had mixed feelings about it.

"Ahkeem I understand that you don't wanna raise another man's baby, but you told me it didn't matter. Am I pissed off? Yes because you prove to me that you are just like the rest." I told him, and his nostrils flared. I was just calling it as I saw it.

"I'm not like the rest, don't you ever compare me to your weak add ex-husband. You know what I'ma let you cool down before we say some things that we will regret. I'm out I'ma call you later." he told me kissing me on the forehead.

I felt like I wasn't saying anything wrong. I mean he was the one that said it didn't matter, but now he wanna know. His insecurities were turning me off, and I could do bad by myself. Getting in the car, I started it and headed back to Shay's place. What turned out to be a good day went left quick. I was wondering if I said something wrong, I needed someone else opinion. Making it inside, I dropped my purse by the door and made my way to the couch. Getting comfortable, I grabbed the remote and turned the tv on. Turning to the food network channel, my stomach growled at the same as my phone rung. Looking at it, I rolled my eyes but answered.

"Hello."

"Kadeem I want you to know I'm sorry if I made you mad today. That was never my intentions."

"Ahkeem it's all good; you didn't make me mad. You showed me the real you, and I appreciate you. What can I do for you though?" I asked him.

"Kadeem this is my baby. I know you haven't ate and I know y'all hungry. Let me feed y'all." He begged, and I gave in.

"Ok give me thirty minutes. Don't think that we are back good; I'm just hungry." I told him, and we shared a laugh. "I'll meet you at Longhorn," I told him and ended the call.

Getting myself together, I turned the tv off and started out the house. When I saw Tyrese, my mood shifted. What could he possibly want? Whatever it was he could save it for someone that wanted to hear it because I damn sure did the.

Chapter 15

Tyrese

The glow that Kadeem has was one that I never seen before. That glow could only mean two thing; she was pregnant or happy with another nigga. If she was pregnant, I wanted to be in my child's life.

"Kadeem let me talk to you for a nigga."

"We don't have shit to talk about. You cheated on me, and we are done. Go ahead and be with your family Tyrese." She told me getting in the car. She tried to close it, but I grabbed it.

"Kadeem know I hurt you and I'm sorry. I never meant for any of this shit to happen." I started, but she stopped me.

"Tyrese save that shit. You made your bed, so you gotta lay in it. I have one question though, why?" She asked with tears running down her face.

"Kadeem I don't know what came over me when I did it, and I wish I could take it back. Angelica was something to do." I told her, and she slapped the shit out of me. And I deserved that.

"But I wasn't there for you. Tyrese get the fuck out the way, I'm on the way somewhere." She told me getting in the car.

I watched her leave, and I felt defeated. I couldn't change any of this, so I decided to give her what she wanted. I decided to sign the divorce papers. She could move on with her life, and I could be in my kids lives. I didn't get a chance to ask her was she pregnant, but I would see her around.

Getting in my car, I drove back to my place. On the drive there, I thought about life. Even though I was losing the best thing that happened to me, I still had Angelica and my kids. I couldn't get rid of her ass even if I paid her. Pulling up to the house, I killed the engine and gathered myself before heading in the house.

"Daddy!" Angel sung as I made it in the house.

I picked her up and kiss her in the face. Yes, I moved them from New York to my place. I mean if we were gonna be a family why not live together.

"Sup baby girl. Look like you missed your daddy. Where your mama at?" I asked her putting her down.

"She's in the bathroom; she's been sick all day." She told me.

"Why you didn't hold her hair while she was throwing up?" I asked her, and she turned up her nose.

"Daddy I don't know what she ate, but it stinks." She informed me holding her nose. I swear she was a messing.

Making my way in the bathroom, Angelica was laying on the bathroom floor naked. By looking at her, I could tell she was exhausted. Picking her up, I gently laid her in the tub and turned the water in. She never opened her eyes while I washed her up. When I was done, I took her out and dried her off. Moving into the room, I laid her in the bed while I got her something to put on. Finding her a nightgown, I walked back over to the bed and put it in her.

"Thank you, Tyrese." She told me.

"You good ma. You want anything to eat?" I asked her, and she turned her nose up.

"Naw I'm good; everything that I eats comes up." She revealed to me.

"You gotta eat something ma. The baby is depending on you. I think you got some left over ginger ale and crackers in there. I'll run and get that." I told her heading out the room.

"Is mommy ok?" Angel asked me as was heading to the kitchen.

"Go see for yourself. Don't be too loud she's resting." I told her as she ran off.

As I was getting the crackers and ginger ale, my phone was ringing off the hook. Whoever it was wasn't giving up. Grabbing the phone out my pocket, I saw that it was Jack.

"Yo man what's good?"

"Tyrese you need to get to the shop, somebody done burnt this bitch down." He told me, and my head started spinning.

I didn't know if any enemies I had. Whoever done this shit was gonna pay, once I found there ass.

"I'm on the way," I told him ending the call.

Taking the stuff in the room, I sat it on the dresser. "Angel take care mama while I'm gone. I'll be right back." I told her, and she nodded.

"Ty where you going?" Angelica asked.

"I'll explain everything when I get back. I can't talk right now." I told her rushing out the house.

When I pulled up to the company, it looked nothing like it used to. There was smoke and ashes everywhere. I wanted to cry so bad but now wasn't the time. The trash company I worked so hard for was hardly recognizable. Exiting my car, I walked over to where Jack was standing.

"Man, what happened?"

"I don't know; they aren't really saying anything." He told me.

"Tyrese Holly?"One of the officer asked, and I nodded. "It look like there was an electrical problem on the inside that caught on fire. I'm sorry this happened to you, but I'm glad you wasn't inside. We are finishing up here and will be out of your hair shortly. Again I'm sorry."He told me before walking off.

I guess this was karma for what I did to my wife. I don't think anything worse could happen to me. I lost my wife and my trash company. Ain't that about a bitch!

Ahkeem

I was sitting in the restaurant waiting for Kadeem; I thought she was gonna stand me up. Looking at the door, I saw her walking in. She looked upset like she had been crying. Getting up, I rushed over to her.

"Everything good Kadeem? Why it look like you been crying?" I asked, and she waved me off.

"I'm good Ahkeem, nothing that I can't handle. Come let's place our order. I'm starving." She informed me, but this wasn't over.

After placing our over, we made our way to the booth. Sitting across the table from her, I couldn't help but stare. Kadeem was so damn beautiful to me, and the fact that she might be carrying my baby was even sexier.

"Didn't your mama teach you that it's not polite to stare?" She asked me, and I laughed.

"My bad ma, you're just so damn beautiful," I told her, and she blushed. "But tell me what's really going on Kadeem. What are we doing?" I asked wanting to know where we stood.

"We are two people having lunch what you mean what we're doing. Do I need to remind you what you did today? I think it's better to leave it where we are friends." She reminded me, and I felt my blood boiling.

"Friends? Naw I can't do that. The feeling that I have for you are more than friends. Thinking about you with another man pisses me off. So you might need to rethink things. This is more than a friendship." I re her pointing between the two of us. Kadeem has shit all twisted.

Nothing else was said as we enjoyed our meal. Kadeem was eating like she was starving, but I blame the baby for that. When we were done, we made small talk. We just talked about life and all that good shit.

"Tyrese came by and saw me today. When I was on the way here, he stopped me outside of Shay's place." She mentioned to me, but I thought I was hearing shit. Did she really say her sorry ass husband stopped by.

"The fuck he wanted?" I asked feeling my face ball up.

"Keem, I don't know. I told his ass to go be with his family because I had somewhere to go." She told me.

"You bout ready to get out of here. Maybe we can go back to my place and watch a movie." I asked her as she was finishing the last of her chicken breast.

"As good as that sound, I'ma face to pass. I'm about to head back to Shay's and take a nap. Maybe another time." She revealed to me taking out her wallet. I looked at her ass like she was crazy.

"Fuck you pulling out your wallet for? Kadeem don't play me like I'm some kinda fuck nigga." I boomed at her.

"watch your tone when you're talking to me Ahkeem. I was just trying to paying for my meal. Fuck this I'm outta here." She told me grabbing her purse and leaving.

After throwing a couple hundreds on the table, I got up and ran behind her. The way she was walking let me know she had an attitude. This was finna be a long pregnancy, and I didn't know how much I could take.

"Kadeem wait up ma. I'm sorry about that; I didn't mean any of that. Forgive me?" I asked her hugging her from behind while nibbling on her ear. A moan slipped out her mouth, letting me know that she wanted it just as much as I did. "Come back to my place, so I can make you feel good," I told her, and she nodded.

"I'll meet you there." She mentioned to me trying to get out of my embrace.

"Naw ride with me, I'll have Hakeem come pick up your car," I told her, and she nodded.

"You better be glad I'm hot and horny. Otherwise, I would've had you beating you dick." She told me heading to the passenger side.

She was crazy as hell if she thought I was finna beat my dick. I stayed with someone on standby when I needed to bust a nut. Until she wanted to do right, I was gonna continue to do me, the fuck she thought.

When we made it to the house, I let us in, and Kadeem went straight to my room. Closing and locking the door, I joined her. Kicking my shoes off, I got in the bed and climbed on top of her careful not to put all my weight on her. Her breathing got shallow that let me know that she indeed wanted the dick. I grabbed her and kissed her lips. She opened her mouth and welcomed my tongue. While sucking on her tongue, my dick was hard as hell wanting to be freed. She reached my dick and released it from my parents. I saw the lust in her eyes. I pulled her dress up and was met by a pretty shaved pussy. I wasted no time chowing down on her wetness.

"Ouuu Ahkeem, I'm about to cum." She moaned as her body shook uncontrollably.

That didn't stop me; I kept sucking until she released a second time. I got up and licked my lips. Kadeem pussy was sweet; I could eat that shit for breakfast, lunch, and dinner.

"You ready for this.?" I asked her stroking my hard poles.

She nodded, and I wasted no time diving deep inside her ocean. I could tell she wasn't fucking anybody by how tight her pussy was. Shit was so wet I had to bite down on my lip so a moan wouldn't slip out. Giving her long strokes, she was scarching my back up. That just let me know I was hitting it right. After not being able to hold it any longer, I bust deep inside her walls. I rolled off of her and onto the bed. As tired as I was my dick got right back hard. Kadeem went to the bathroom, and I heard the shower come on. I wanted to join her, but my body wouldn't let me get up.

"Where you going?" I asked Kadeem as she strolled in the room putting her clothes back on.

"Thanks for the dick, but I gotta get home. I'll call you when I get there." She told he exiting my room.

Damn her ass played me, she only wanted me for my dick. I felt defeated; I let her go. Closing my eyes, I drifted off to sleep thinking about how I could get back good with Kadeem.

Chapter 16

Kadeem

"What's wrong boo? You been sulking ever since you came home." Shay asked me.

"To tell you the truth, I didn't know what wrong. I fault myself for what happened between Ty and I. Ahkeem is there, but I can't deal with another heartbreak. I'ma raise my child and work on me." I told her rubbing my belly.

"Kadeem see that's your first problem; you can't blame yourself for what happened between y'all. He did that while you was at home catering to him. Point blank period, he's a man and men are gonna do what they wanna do. Now as for Ahkeem, don't take it out on him. Get to know him; he looks like he's an amazing man. I know that Hakeem is. I know before you say anything it's not what it seem. Shay don't catch feelings, but Hakeem changed that for me. I could possibly be in love with him, but it's too soon to tell. I guess I'm enjoying life." She told me with a shrug.

"Damn girl I'm so happy for you." I beamed.

"Thank you, baby. I just didn't think nan nigga would change me, but talk to me. What's on your mind?"

"You know when I first found out I was pregnant, I didn't and still don't know who the father is. Tyrese still don't know, and Ahkeem told me he was gonna be there no matter what. Then his tune switched up at the doctor appointment. He wants a paternity test before the baby comes, but told me he's gonna be there no matter what. He sends me mixed feelings, and I don't like it. Hell if I would've wanted that, I would've stayed with Ty cheating ass." I told her, and she gave me a weird look. A look that I have never seen before. "Shay, what was that look for?"

"Kadeem I don't want you to get mad; just hear me out." She told me as she took a deep breath. "About a week ago, I was coming to y'all house to check on you and Ty was standing outside talking to some woman. They were in a heated argument and didn't see me. I couldn't figure out what they were say, but Ty dismissed her and told her not to ever come around there again. You know me, I followed her ass, and she ended up at the hotel that we went to. I put two and two together when I saw the little girl get out the car. I wanted to tell you, but I didn't want to see you get hurt." She told me, and I was livid. She was my best friend, how Gould she not tell me some shot like that.

"Really Shay! You was supposed to be my best damn friend, and you hid some shit like this. A best friend wouldn't do dime shit like that. I guess I don't know your ass like I thought I did. I'm out; please don't call me or try to find me." I told her getting up and running out the house.

Shay and I have been friends forever, and her hiding something like this has fucked me up. When I made it to the car, I let the tears fall freely. I was so hurt and betrayed. I crunk up the car up and drove off with no destination in mind. All I knew was, I needed to get the fuck away from everybody, I needed to be alone right now.

Two and half hours later, I was reading a sign saying Waycross Georgia. I would have been there soon, but I kept stopping for food and to stretch. I had no one there, but I was finna enjoy myself. Pulling up to the nearest hotel, I exited the car and headed inside.

"Welcome to Hilton Inn, I'm Molly, and I'm here to assist you today." The receptionist greeted me as soon as I walked in.

"Hey Molly, I need a room for a week."

"Yes, ma'am! I need your id and will you be needing a single or double bed."

Single is fine; here you go." I handed her my license. "Can I possibly get a room on the second floor?" I asked, and she nodded.

I left everything at home, so I would need to go shopping tomorrow. After giving me my key, I headed to my room and got comfortable. My phone was buzzing off the hook. I had over thirty missed calls from Shay, and fifteen from Ahkeem. I turned it off and got comfortable on the bed before drifting off. I didn't have shit to say to nobody right now!

Shay

"I've been calling Kadeem like crazy and still nothing. I know I was wrong for not telling her, but I thought I was doing the right thing by not telling her. I think I lost my best friend for good." I vented to Hakeem.

We were sitting at my crib kicking it, but I missed Kadeem something serious. I loved Hakeem company, but I wanted Kadeem because she got me.

"Give her some time; she's be back. You drop a bombshell on her, you can't expect her not to be mad. If she's a real best friend, she'll be back." Hakeem assured me, and I hope he was right.

The rest of the day, Hakeem and I laid around talking. My mind wondered off to Kadeem and wondered if she was ok. I grabbed my phone and dialed her only to get the voicemail. I was worried not only for her but for the baby as well.

I decided to let her be, and when she was ready, she would reach out. I never meant to keep anything from her, but at the same time, I didn't want her to get hurt either just as I was about to get ready to shower, my phone rung. I ran over to it and low and behold it was Kadeem.

"Hello," I answered out of breath.

"I was calling to let you know that I will be over in a couple of days to get my clothes. I will also be bringing your key back. I think that it's best for me to deal with things on my own."

"Kadeem why are you doing me like this. I said I was sorry; what more can I do?"

"Just let me be! You hurt me by hiding that from me. If it were me that saw that shit, I would've been trying to break my neck to get to you. I see where your loyalty lies." She told me hanging up.

This wasn't my best friend, and I could tell that this was hurting her just as it was hurting me. I just couldn't believe that she would throw away years of friendship over this bullshit. I mean I know I was wrong, but damn she could cut me some damn slack.

I threw my phone on the bed and got ready for bed. I would just give her some time, and if it's meant to be, it would be. If not fuck it! Getting comfortable in the bed, I drifted off to sleep!

Chapter 17

Ahkeem

"Kadeem, where the hell are you?" I boomed into the phone.

"I needed to get my mind right, so I disappeared for a while. Just know that I'm straight though," She told me calm as hell.

"Kadeem, have you been to the doctor? I'm worried about you," I told her sincerely. Hell, I was that was my child too!

"My appointment is next week, and I'd rather go by myself," She told me, but that wasn't happening.

"Not happening! I don't give a fuck what you're going through; you ain't finna keep me from my baby."

"Oh, so it's your baby now, huh? The other day you was just asking for a paternity test. Make up your fucking mind. You're too grown to be acting like a little ass boy." She matched my tone.

"Kadeem, I'm sorry about that. I never meant to make you feel any kinda way. I want this baby just as much as you do. I don't give a damn about no paternity test, just let me come to where you are. I need you, Kadeem," I told her, sounding like a little bitch.

"I'll let you know the date and time of the appointment, but I can't let you know where I am. I feel that this is the best for both of us. Give me some time to think, and once I'm ready, we will talk. I'm hurting right now, and I need to heal on my own," she told me, and I heard the pain in her voice when she said everything. I wondered what all this was about.

"Cool," was all I said before hanging up.

"Nigga, what the fuck is wrong with you?" Hakeem walked in the door and asked me.

"Man, I don't know. Kadeem is sending me mixed feelings. One minute I want a paternity test for the baby she carryin', and the next I don't. I told her that I would be there for them no matter what, but I don't even believe that myself. If that baby ain't mine, I don't think that I would be able to raise another man's baby. I'm confused as fuck to what is going on and why she left though," I told Hakeem.

"I know what you mean, but why did you tell her that knowing that you wasn't telling her the truth? You should have been straight up with her, the same shit I told Shay. If Shay would've told her about her husband, then Kadeem would've still been here. Give her a minute to take all this in, and she will be back," he told me, and I raised my brow.

"What do you mean if Shay would have told her about her husband? Nigga, talk to me."

"I don't know all about it; Shay just gave me the shorter version of it. Apparently, Shay knew that her husband was cheating and didn't tell her. They got in this argument, and Kadeem left. I told Shay that she should have told her as soon as it happened, and she said that it slipped her mind. Ain't no way in hell something like that just magically slips your mind. Like I told her, she made that bed, so it's only right for her to lay in it. I had to leave that bitch because she over there in her damn feelings."

"Damn, I didn't know about all that shit either. I guess it's only right to let shit cool down. I just hate to see her hurting like that. I think a nigga might be in love." I told him, and he chuckled.

"Nigga, I could've been told your ass that. I just never seen your ass like this before. Shit, I'ma finna get ready to head to the gym. From the looks of things, your ass need to be doin' the same," he told me before walking off.

Yeah, I done gained a little weight, but I was nowhere near sloppy. I got my ass up and headed to the kitchen to find me something to eat. I gave Bonney the day off, so I was on my own for the day. After making me a sandwich and grabbing me a Gatorade, I headed in the living room and turned the tv on. Before I started eating my sandwich, I decided to text Kadeem.

Me: I never meant for you to feel any kinda way. To tell the truth, I think I love your ass. I have never in life been like this with any female. You are special to a nigga, please don't push me away. I know you feel what I feel.

Baby Mama: Ahkeem, I knew that it was something special with you, but I'm protecting my heart. It has been through enough shit, and I don't think I can take anything else like that. I want to give you my all, but I'm afraid that it's not gonna be enough. Please let me be, and if God sees fit, we will be together. I got to get my life right first before I can love again. I hope you understand.

Damn that was some deep shit. I decided to let it be and pray that God saw fit for Kadeem and I to be together. After eating my sandwich, I got myself together to hit the gym. Throwing on my ballers and a beater, I grabbed my keys and headed out the day. On the drive to the gym, I blasted "Nameless" by Lil' Keed. It was something about that song that always got me pumped. When I first heard the song, I was wondering why it was called nameless, but the more I listened to it, I understood why. Pulling up at the gym, I grabbed my wireless headphone sand turned them on. Turning on my Apple Music, I decided to listen to Kevin Gates. Strolling in the gym, I gave them my key, and they told me to have a good workout. Yep, I was finna get it in. Heading to the treadmill, I stepped on and turned it on. Raising the speed to five, I got it in. When I was finished, I wiped my machine off and headed straight for the weights.

"Hey Ahkeem," Molly spoke, and I gave her ass the head nod. I wasn't checking for her ass like that no more. I had one woman on mind and one woman only.

Once I was finished at the gym, I got in my car and headed home. On the drive, I got a weird feeling in my stomach, one of which I never felt before. Making it to the house, I jumped out the car and ran in the house. Opening the door, I met Bonney on the floor. From the looks of things, it looked like she had been there for a minute. I bent down and checked for a pulse, and it was very faint. If anything happened to Bonney, I would lose my mind. Scooping her up, I ran out to the car and put her in.

"Stay with me, Bonney, don't you die on me!" I hollered before getting in the driver's seat.

Speeding to the hospital as fast as I could, I prayed that Bonney was good. Upon making it there, I parked the car and took Bonney out the back seat. Her body was cold, and that only meant one thing, but I wasn't gonna believe it until the doctor told me.

"I need some help over here!" I screamed, holding Bonney in my arms.

"Sir, can you tell me what happened?" one of the nurses asked.

"When I came home from the gym, I found her laying on the floor by the door. From my knowledge, she didn't have any health issues. Please help her," I told her, handing her to the nurse.

"Don't worry we will do the best we can to save her. Have a seat and the doctor will come talk to you when we get her stable." She told me, and I nodded.

Grabbing my phone, I dialed Hakeem and waited for him to pick up. "Nigga get to the hospital; it's Bonney." Was all I said before I ended the call.

My nerves were getting the best of me. I couldn't sit still, so I got up and paced the floor. People were looking at me like I was crazy, but I didn't give a shit. About 15 minutes later, Hakeem came running through the door. He rushed over to me and pulled me in for a hug. Bonney was like a grandmother to us. She cleaned, cooked and did everything she could for us.

"Family of Bonney Hughes."

"Yes." I ran over to where the lady was standing.

"I'm sorry for your loss. We did all we could; she was dead when she came in. From the looks of things, she had a massive heart attack. You couldn't save her even if you wanted to; her heart was already weak. You can see her if you like before we take her to the morgue. Again, I'm sorry." She told us, and I broke down. I didn't know that Bonney had any heart problems. Looking at her she looked as healthy as a horse. This had really fucked me up, and I didn't know what I was gonna do without her.

"Ahkeem, it's gonna be alright bruh. Just think about her as being in better place. Bonney wouldn't want us carrying on like this. Get yourself together, so we can go say our last goodbyes." Keem told me, and he was right.

After getting myself together, I followed the doctor down the hall. When we made it to Bonney's room, I said a quick prayer before walking in. Looking over at Bonney, she looked like she was sleeping so peaceful. She didn't have to suffer no more; she was in a better place. We walked over to her bedside, and I leaned down and kissed her on the forehead.

"Damn Bonney, you fucked me up with this one. Why didn't you tell us that you were having heart problems? We could have brought you another one. You might be gone Bonney, but you will never be forgotten." I told her kissing her one last time before walking out the room.

We were all Bonney had so we had to figure out what we were gonna do about a funeral. She told us all the time that when she died, she wanted to be cremated and wanted her ashes spread over Tybee Island. I thought she was crazy when she said that because I never thought that we had to do this so soon. I mean if that's what she wanted, that's what we would be doing. I needed to get away from the hospital, so I shot Keem a message and told him I was headed home.

Today was a rather sad day. I lost someone that meant so much to me. It was gonna be hard being in the house without Bonney. If Kadeem ever got her mind right, I would sell this house and move us in another house. I wanted to call her but decided against it. Making it to the house, I walked in an felt a cold breeze fly past me. Bonney would forever be in my heart. Going to her room, I walked in and laid on her bed. Bonney's bed was so comfortable. Within a matter of minutes, I had done drifted off to sleep.

Kadeem one month later

I was finna back in Savannah for good. I missed everything about home. Shay and I were back friends and boy was I glad. The time that I spent away, I reflected on life and what I had to live for. I hate that I wasn't there for Ahkeem when Bonney died, but he knew why. The divorce had finally gone through, and it felt like a burden lifted off my shoulders. The lawyers told me that the house and the car belonged to me, but I didn't want shit from Tyrese. He paid for them, so it was only right for him to keep them. I didn't want anything to tie me to him. I was at a place in life where things were finally starting to look up for me. I had finally found a house in the country part of Savannah that I was expecting to move in next week. I had so much to do before my baby got here. Ahkeem and I decided to work on us to see where it was go.

"Bae, what you over there thinking about?" Akeem broke me out of my thoughts. He was looking sexy as ever.

"Life, and how blessed I am. I'm a free woman, and I thank the lord for that."

"I hear you, baby. I'm glad that you came to your senses and came back to a nigga. I was losing my mind without your ass. Promise me that whatever we go through, you won't leave a nigga again."

"I promise, only if you don't give me a reason too. As long as you keep us happy, then you have nothing to worry about." I told him rubbing my belly.

"Oh, you have nothing to worry about. I'ma keep that pretty smile on your face for the rest of my life. What you got planned today?" he asked me, and I shrugged.

"Nothing. I planned to lay here and sleep all day. I'm tired." I told him being dramatic.

"What if your man wanted to take you out tonight? I want to show you off baby." He told me licking his lips. Damn this man was so damn sexy.

"Everybody knows me here. Ain't nobody thinking about me." I told him, and he got close to me and whispered in my ear.

"I ain't talking about here baby. I wanna take you out of Savannah, just you and me."

"What you got in mind?" I asked him with a raise of my brow.

"Shit I was thinking that we can go to Cancun. I could use this, and I'm sure you can too. Let your man give you the world." He told me. I bit my lip and clenched my thighs. This man was something els, and I was thankful for him.

"Sounds good. When are we leaving?" I asked.

"1:00." He told me, and I looked at his ass like he was crazy. It was already 11:00 and I haven't even packed yet. My hair was all over my head. There was no way that I was gonna be ready by one. "I see the wheels over there turning. Don't worry when we get there, I'ma take you shopping. You can call Shay over and get that head of your right. No way in hell you gonna be following behind me like that." He told me, and I playfully hit him. "I'm just fucking with you baby. You're my queen, and I don't care if your hair all over your head." He told me kissing my lips.

"Aww thank you baby, but you right. Let me call Shay and see if she can get me right. Thank you for making me so happy baby." I told him.

"No thanks needed. Hurry up we don't wanna miss our flight." He told me, and I grabbed my phone.

"Hey, girl. I need a favor; I need my hair slaved to the Gods." I told her as soon as she answered the phone.

"Say no more. Give me about 15 minutes, and I'm on the way. What's the occasion?"

"Bitch I'm going to Cancun!" I screamed into phone.

"Damn bitch, you know what I'm on the way now. I'll see you when I get there." She told me ending the call.

Shay was so damn extra, but I don't know what I would do without her. I got up and headed to the bathroom to handle my hygiene. Ahkeem was in his office doing god knows what. Once I was finished, I turned the tv on and turned it to the lifetime channel. Ahkeem hated the movies on Lifetime. Talking about most of them are staged, well they were some good ass staged movies. Just as I got comfortable on the chair, I heard a knock at the door. I knew it was Shay ass, so I hollered come in.

"Hey girl!" she walked in and hugged me.

"Hey boo. How is life treating you? I'm loving that glow." I told her, and she blushed.

"Me too. I'm loving life, and I have Hakeem to thank for that. Enough about me though. How is my little peanut doing?" she asked rubbing my stomach.

"All is well. It's growing good, and I can't wait to find out what it is. Ahkeem swears it's a girl, but I think it's a boy."

"That's my little princess in there." Ahkeem walked up to me and rubbed my belly. "Sup Shay. Please hurry up and get this head right." He told her laughing. I gave him the look, and he stopped. "I'm just fucking with you baby. You know that I love you." He tole me kissing my lips.

"Baby I'm so happy for you. This is a long time coming. I want you to go to Cancun and enjoy yourself. You can't come back pregnant because you already are." She told me, and I shrugged.

It took Shay about an hour to do my hair. I swear her hands were gifted, my sew in looked like I had just come from the shop. Thanking her, she left out, and I went to take a quick shower. We had about 45 minutes to make it to the Airport. Jumping in the shower, I washed up and jumped out as quick as I jumped in. Walking over to Ahkeem's closet, I grabbed a pair of his sweats and laid them on the bed. I wore them because they were so comfortable. Whenever we get to Cancun, I would get sexy.

"Kadeem we need be rolling out baby." Ahkeem hollered from downstairs.

"I'm coming baby. I'm throwing on my clothes now." I yelled back, and I heard him suck his teeth.

Five minutes later, I was rushing downstairs. Ahkeem looked at me and shook his head. "It's about time you came down. You look comfortable as fuck." He told me looking me up and down. Everything that I had on was his other than my bra and underwear.

"Sorry baby, your clothes shouldn't be so comfortable. Come on before we miss our flight and I'ma be mad." I told him walking out the door.

Ahkeem walked to my door and opened it for me, once I was in, he shut it and walked around to his side. I was excited to get away from Savannah for a while, but I was ecstatic to be going to Cancun. I heard that it was nice, and I couldn't wait to see for myself. On the ride, somehow, I drifted off to sleep. I swear this baby was draining me and I couldn't wait to have it. This was only the beginning to something special.

Chapter 18

Ahkeem

I was happy to have my lady back in my life. Kadeem was it for me. I told her that I wanted to take her out and show her the world. I meant just that. Hakeem had gone to Cancun before us to set up our special day. I knew it seemed like it was too early, but I couldn't see me without Kadeem. Those couple weeks that she was gone, I thought I was gonna lose my mind. I couldn't lose her again, and in Cancun, I planned to pop the question. Yeah, you heard me right, my player days were gone. I looked over in the passenger seat, and it looked like she was sleeping so peacefully, slob falling from her mouth and everything.

"Baby, get up. We're here," I told her, shaking her a little.

"I'm up," she told me, wiping the slob from her mouth. All I could do was laugh.

We got out and headed into the airport. After getting our tickets, we waited to board the plane. I grabbed Kadeem's hand and gave it a light squeeze. "You ready for this baby?" I asked her.

"Ready as I'll ever be." She told me, and I smiled.

As we waited, I texted Hakeem back in forth to make sure that everything was in order. I was nervous as hell because I had no idea what she was gonna say. She could only say yes or no. I would be heartbroken if she told me, no, but I would have to deal with it. Just thinking about her saying no had me all in my feelings.

"Flight board for Cancun is loading now." Was called over the intercom. I grabbed Kadeem's hand, and we headed over to the attendant.

We got on the flight and buckled up. Kadeem laid her head on my shoulder, and I knew what time it was. I knew that she was gonna be out before we got up in the air. Thanks to the baby, she was always sleeping. So this trip was much needed. Five hours later, we were landing in Cancun Mexico, and I couldn't wait to be on the beach drinking me a pineapple drink.

"Come on bae; lets get a car so we can head to the hotel. Once we get checked in, I'll take you shopping. Is that cool baby?" I asked, and she nodded.

"Whatever you wanna do baby."

"Naw the world is yours; I'm only living in it," I told her, and she blushed. Days like these I wish I could cherish forever.

When we made it to the hotel, we checked in and headed to the room. I couldn't wait to see her face once she walked in the room. Making it to the room, I gave Kadeem a key, and she opened the door. As soon as she opened it, the waterworks started. Hakeem had hooked the room up; he had rose petals everywhere. Not to mention he had a bowl of chocolate covered strawberries by the bed. I knew that was one of Kadeem's favorite fruit.

"Ahkeem how did you did all this? Thank you so much. I love it." She told me kissing me.

"Don't worry your pretty self; I'm glad you like it though. Come on let's relax for a bit and I'ma take you shopping as promise. I got your favorite fruit, come on and laid down, so

I can feel them to you." I told her, and she jumped on the bed.

"Ahkeem you are heaven sent. Thank you for making this special, but I wanna know how you did it."

"If I told you, I would have to kill you," I told her chuckling. "I'm just fucking with you. I know people that know people. I called in a few favors and boom this happened." I told her holding out my arms.

As promised I fed Kadeem strawberries until her stomach hurt. After she was good and full of strawberries y'all knew what she wanted to do. Yep, she wanted to sleep. As bad as I wanted to be deep inside her tunnel, I decided to let her rest because tonight it was on and popping. If she wasn't already pregnant, she would've been tonight. As Kadeem laid on the bed, I thought that it would be an good idea if I caught up on some much-needed sleep as well. Kicking off my shoes, I grabbed her and pull her on my chest. I wanted her close to my heart where she belonged. Closing my eyes, I let sleep come over me.

I was woken up out of my sleep with my phone going off in my pocket. I silenced it so that I wouldn't wake Kadeem up. Easing it out of my pocket, I saw that Hakeem was texting me. Probably telling that everything was in place. I opened the message and that exactly what he was telling me. I eased from under Kadeem and went to handle my hygiene. We still had shopping to do before I popped the question. Once I was done in the bathroom, I grabbed Kadeem's phone and set her alarm to wake her up in an hour. Grabbing a pen and paper, I wrote her a note on what to do when she woke up. I still had a couple things to do before we met up tonight. Kissing her on the forehead, I grabbed my wallet and exited the room. Tonight was gonna be a night to remember.

*****

Kadeem

What the fuck I thought when I got up to my alarm going off. I reached on the other side of the bed, and Ahkeem was laying beside me. I jumped up and headed to the bathroom to relieve my bladder. After washing my hands, I walked out of the bathroom puzzled. Looking on the nightstand, I saw a note. I picked it up and read it.

You were sleeping so peaceful that I didn't want to wake you. Handle your hygiene, and a car will be out waiting for you to take you shopping. Something came up, but I will see you tonight. I love you ma.

I placed the letter back on the dresser and did what was asked of me. Hell, I didn't have any clothes here, so I had to wear what I had on. I saw on the bed clueless to that Ahkeem had to do so important to leave me in the room alone. In the middle of my thoughts, there was a knock at the door, I grabbed my bag and walked to the door. Standing on my tippy toes, I pecked out the hole. I saw someone holding a banquet of flowers. Opening the door, I was greeted with the flowers.

"Kadeem?" she asked.

"Yes, that's me."

"These are for you and your car is waiting downstairs for you." She told me handing me the flowers.

"Thank you. I'll be right down." I told her closing the door. Grabbing the note, I sat the flowers on the table.

These are for my beautiful lady. Head on out and get something nice. Don't worry about spending too much; I want you to enjoy yourself. When you get to the car, call me. Love Ahkeem.

I wondered what the hell he had under his sleeve. I grabbed my phone and exited the room. When I made it downstairs, an older gentleman was waiting for me with a sign. I thought that was hilarious. I walked over to the car, and he opened the door for me. I climbed in, and he shut the door. I felt like royalty. When he got in the car, he handed me the black card. I gladly took it and put it in my purse. There was a bowl of strawberry and a couple bottle of water on the other side of the car. Ahkeem was so thoughtful. I grabbed the strawberries and started eating them; I washed them down with a bottle of water. When my baby come out it gonna be looking like a strawberry. I swear that was all I wanted these days.

"We are here, go ahead and enjoy your shopping. I'll be here waiting when you return." He told me helping me out the car.

After thanking him, I headed inside the mall. It was much nicer than the ones back home. I felt like I had died and went to heaven. I was in dire need of a manicure and a pedicure, so that was my first stop.

"Welcome to La La's! What can we do for you today?"

"Yes, I need a pedicure and a full set," I told her looking at all the pretty colors. They had some colors that I had never seen before.
"When you find your color, you can have a seat at the first station and Jia will assist you. Can I get you anything to drink?" she asked me.

"I'll take a bottle of water please," I told her.

I decided to get the ombre nails and orange on my toes. Once I had my color, I went over to the first station like she told me. Taking my shoes and socks off, I stuck my feet in the water. Yes, lord, this is just what I needed. The water was just right. Then when she started massaging them was everything. From the temperature of the water and the way she was massaging my feet, I kinda drifted off to sleep. I was woken by a tap on my arm, telling me that she was finished. My toes were so damn people. I couldn't wait to find me some shoes to show them off. After she was done with my nails, I felt whole again. I never went anywhere without my nails and feet done. Thanking them, I exited out the shop.

Keem: I can't wait to see you tonight. Have you found something to wear yet?

Me: Just leaving the nail shop, I'm heading there now.

Keem: Cool meet me at the address at 8:30.

Just as the address came through, I moved into Guess. I loved me some Guess. Strolling the racks, I found a couple pair of shorts, shirts, swimsuits, a dress, sandals, heels. Ahkeem told me to ball out, so that's what the fuck I was finna do. I only spent $4,000; I didn't wanna hurt his card. Once I was done, I grabbed my phone and called Ahkeem. There was no way in hell I was gonna be able to carry all these damn bags.

"Baby I need some help with these bags, I think I went a little overboard," I told him once he picked up the phone.

"Let me call the driver, what store you in? Don't be trying to carry all dem damn bags." He fussed.

"I'm in Guess. Tell him to hurry up my feet hurts." I whined.

"Say less, he on the way baby. Love you." He told hanging up.

What seem like forever, the driver finally showed up. He grabbed my bags, and I headed to the car. He looked like he was struggling, but Keem told me not to be handling them bag. He didn't have to tell me twice. When I looked at my phone, it was a quarter after six. The time wasn't waiting for nobody. Making it to the car, I climbed in and got comfortable. My stomach growled telling me that it was time to eat. I didn't know what Ahkeem had planned, but I hope it was something dealing with food because I was starving.

Making it back to the hotel, I headed up to the room. I didn't even wait for the driver; I had to pee so bad. When I made it inside the room, I closed and locked the door. I was here alone, and I wasn't risking it. I mean the people seemed nice here, but you couldn't put it, past people, these days. After relieving my bladder, I headed back to the door and opened it.
"I'm sorry about that. You can place the bags right there. Thank you." I told him as he placed the bags on the table.

"The pleasure is mine. Have a wonderful night." He told me leaving out the room.

Once he was gone, I took my clothes off and headed into the bathroom to shower. After tying my hair up, I turned the water on and got in the shower. The water was at the perfect temperature; I could stay in here all night. Taking my sponge, I put some body wash on it, and I started washing my body. While I was in my phone went off, I knew it was one of the two, Shay or Ahkeem. They would just have to wait until I got out the shower. When I felt squeaky clean, I got out and grabbed a towel. Once I was done drying off, I headed back in my room and grabbed my phone.

Best friend: How is Cancun? I wish I could be there with you but enjoy your man.

Me: It's nice! Girl, I'm tired as hell. Ahkeem sent me shopping, and I got my toes and feet done. Talking about he will see me later tonight. I wonder what the hell he got up his sleeve.

Best Friend: Well enjoy yourself. I'll see you when you get you get back. I love you.

I proceeded to get ready for tonight. I grabbed the lotion and spread it all over my body. I picked out a simple yet cute yellow dress. I had the wedges to match the dress; my jewelry was simple. I had a necklace and matching earrings. Taking the scarf off my head, I fingered the curls. I must say Shay had me looking like money. In the middle of taking a selfie, the room phone rung.

"Hello."

"Kadeem, you have a message at the front desk." Was all the person said before hanging up.

I put the phone down and looked at my phone. It was a fifteen minutes till eight, so I decided to head on down to the lobby. I had no idea how long it was going to take to get to the address that Ahkeem texted me. Gathering my thing, I walked out the room and shut the door. Getting to the lobby, I walked up to the desk and waited for the lady to get off the phone.

"I'm Kadeem, and I was told there was a message here for me."

"Here you go, ma'am. Enjoy your night." She told me handing me an envelope.

The time has come, and I can't wait to see you. I hope that today was everything and more. I'll see you in a bit. Love Ahkeem. P.S. I hope you got an appetite!

After reading the note, I blushed. Ahkeem was everything that I could want in a man. He caters to my every need, and he's right there when I needed him. Sticking the note in my bad, I thanked the lady and headed out the door. It night skies was so pretty, and I couldn't wait to see what tonight consist of in Cancun. Walking over to the car, the driver opened the door for me, and I slid in. The driver got in and drove off. It took forever, but we pulled up to this fancy restaurant called Grand Luxe. I opened the door and got out. Making it inside, I saw Ahkeem looking good enough to eat. I ran over to him and hugged him. He picked me up and spun me around. I was in heaven when I was in his arms.

"Look like somebody missed me," he told, and I hit him in the chest.

"How dare you leave me all day? You told me you were gonna take me shopping today, and I had to go all alone." I told him pouting.

"I'm sorry, I wanted our first night in Cancun to be special. So while you were shopping, I was setting all this up." He told me pointing around the restaurant.

I must say he had done a good job. There were candles and roses everywhere, but I know that he didn't do this on his own. He had to have had help; everything was so neat and pretty. Blackstreet Boys Before I let you go was playing. One of my favorite songs of all times.
"Can I have this dance?" he asked, and I nodded like a school. He grabbed my hand and pulled me to him. Being in his arms were where I wanted to be all day. He grabbed my

hips, and we slow danced to the song. He sung to me and it made my heart melt. The tears were slipping from my eyes before I knew it.

I don't wanna lose your love, mmm

I don't wanna say bye-bye, oh no no

True love is so hard to find

And it's right between your lips and mine, and mine

"Baby don't cry! It was never my intentions to fall for you as hard as I did. Kadeem, I can't live without you, and I shouldn't have to. When I look in your eyes, I see our future. I see us in our new home with our kids running around the house tearing up shit." He stopped laughing. "No for real, Kadeem I can't see me without you in my life. I never really understood the value of life, until you walked into it. Baby, I want this forever. Will you do me the honor and marry me?" he asked me dropping down on one knee.

My throat got tight, and all I could do was nod. I just gotten out of a marriage, and I really hope this was gonna be my last. I was taking back by all this; I didn't know he was bringing me here to propose to me. I thought we were just coming to enjoy ourselves and get away from everything. "Yes I will marry you, but promise me that you won't hurt me," I told him with tears streaming down my face. He took his hand and wiped them away.

"I can't promise that I won't hurt you. I'ma man and I make mistakes, you never have to worry about me cheating or hurting you. I won't be perfect, but when I leave to go somewhere, you won't have to worry about me fucking off on you. I vow to love you the way that you suppose to be love, do things to your body that you never felt before. I wanna give you the world Kadeem." He told me smiling. "She said yes, y'all can come out now." He hollered, and Shay and Hakeem appeared.

"I hate you. You knew 'bout this all along and did even tell me." I told Shay hugging her neck.

"As bad as I wanted to tell you, I couldn't mess this day up for you. Look at you; you look so damn happy." She told me.

"Congratulations sis in law. Welcome to the family. I'm happy for y'all. My brother been through a lot of shit and he need somebody like you in his life. When you disappeared for a while, this nigga went crazy. I thought he was gonna lose his shit." He told me laughing. "No for real I'm glad you came back. I thought I was gonna have to admit his ass in an institution. I love you bruh, but tell me that I'm lying."

"Nigga, please. I mean I was going crazy, but the institution shit, naw. I'm glad she came back though, and I ain't never letting her go." He told me hugging me from behind.

"You don't have to worry about me leaving if you keep showing me this side of you. No, I just playing, I love you baby and thank you for making me so happy. Can we eat now? I'm starving? Them strawberries that you were feeding me all day are gone. I need some meat in my life." I told him.

"I got some meat for you baby." He whispered in my ear. "No, come on let me feed y'all." He told me leading me to the table.

The rest of the night, we ate and enjoyed each other company. I was gonna get shay back for hiding this from me. This night couldn't get any better; I was engaged and happy. I couldn't wait to start my forever with Ahkeem. After dinner, I was stuff. All I could think about was my head hitting the pillow. Of course, my fiancé had other plans. I saw the lust in his eyes when he looked at me, and I felt my pussy pulsing just thinking about him stroking me.

"Well, we finna head back to the room. I'm finna make love to my fiancé." He told his brother and Shay. I elbowed him. "What! You wanted me to lie and tell them that we were finna go to bed. That's the last thing on my mind right now. I'm finna get all up in them guts." He told me, and Hakeem dapped him up.

"My nigga! Go handle your business bruh. We finna go do the same thing. Congratulations again." Hakeem told us.

"Alright boo, I'll get up with you tomorrow," I told Shay hugging her.

As expected, Ahkeem and I almost didn't make it to the hotel. When we got in the room, he pulled my dress up and started giving me long deep strokes. We didn't make it to the bed, and I wasn't mad. I was letting my fiancé do whatever he wanted to my body. All you could hear throughout the room was our body slapping together and my moaning. I hated it for the people in the rooms next to us because they were gonna hear me all night. I would apology tomorrow, but I'm sure they would understand.

"Oh my God Ahkeem, fuck your pussy baby." I moaned as he was tapping my insides.

"Baby I love you so much. Lay on the bed so that I can make love to you." He told me as I rushed over to the bed and spread my legs as wide as I could. He wasted no time diving in wetness.

The rest of the night, we made love and ate strawberries. I couldn't wait to see where life took us.

Epilogue (One year later)

Kadeem

"Mya, get down before you fall. You would not be doing this if your daddy was here," I told her as she jumped off the chair. This child was gonna be the death of me. She was my little daredevil.

"Again, again!" She clapped as she went and got back on the chair. When her little ass fall and hurt herself, she would sit down. A hard head makes a soft ass.

Yes, Mya was Ahkeem's, she looked just like his ass. From her big eyes to his good hair. The other thing she had of mine was her skin complexion. No paternity test was needed. He told me that he was gonna be there for me no matter what, and he kept his promise. Today was Mya's birthday, and we were waiting for Ahkeem to come back so that we could start the party. Ahkeem rented bounce house, cotton candy machines, got a clown, the whole nine yards. It was just us and Shay them. Shay ass had popped out a baby right after me, and I never knew that her ass was pregnant. She kept that shit a secret, and I wasn't mad at her. She had a little boy that she named Hakeem Jr, and him and Mya were thick as thieves. When they got in trouble, they did that shit together.

"Happy Birthday, happy birthday to you." Shay sung as she walked into the house. Mya ran over to Hakeem and damn near knocked him down. All I could do was laugh; she didn't acknowledge Shay. "Auntie don't get no love." She pouted as she held out her arms.

"Nope, come on Keem." She grabbed him and pulled him to the back yard.

"I swear her little ass is hell, and you sure you ready for another one," Shay asked hugging me.

"Do it look like I have a choice. After this one, I'm done. Keem ain't getting no more baby out of me." I started, and Ahkeem walked in the house.

"Why not? You told me that you would give me as many as I wanted and I want at least three more." He told me walking into the kitchen with the cake.

"Boy, you done fell and bumped your head if you think I'm about to have three more children. Mya already bad as hell, and I feel like Jr gonna be the same one. When I have him, I'ma get my tubes tied, burnt, and clipped." I told him, and Shay was rolling, but I was dead ass serious.

"Stop lying hoe; you know that you gonna give him another one. Let me get out her and check on these kids. They will be done deflated the bounce house, y'all know they bad as hell together." Shay told us, and I nodded.

"How you feeling baby?" Ahkeem asked me as he placed a wet kiss on my lips. My pussy lips responded. I was in no predicament to be thinking about dick right now. I was eight months pregnant and over it all.

"Big as hell. Look at me, I look like a damn whale, what you mean how I feel. I'm over this damn pregnancy. I don't remember it being this bad when I was pregnant with Mya. I can't wait to have his ass; you better be glad I love you ass because I wouldn't have gotten pregnant so quick after I had her." I fussed.

"I'm sorry you having a bad day, but we gotta get though Mya's birthday. Come on, let's go get some sun. I'ma give you a full body massage tonight when Mya go to sleep; that's the least I can do." He told me helping me up from the couch. I must say that my husband was good to me.

We went outside and joined the party. I didn't do much walking because my feet were on swole. I couldn't see my ankles, and I couldn't wait to be able to lay on my stomach again. It was hot as hell out for it to be June. I couldn't wait for some cooler weather. I love seeing Mya and Ahkeem interact. She was the true definition of a daddy's girl. Ahkeem and I couldn't even watch a movie together, and he little butt had to be in the middle. I wouldn't trade them for nothing in the world though.

"Where Hakeem at Shay?" I asked her as she sat down in the chair beside me.

"He pose to be on his way; you know his ass gotta be extra. Talking about he was going to Toys R Us to get Mya some toys." She told me, and I laughed.

"Tell Hakeem don't be bring all that shit over here, y'all might as well take it home with y'all. Her room is already full of toys. Every time we go to the store, she thinks she supposed to get something. Of course, she has her daddy wrapped around her finger, so he give in. Me on the other hand, I just let her little ass cry." I told her with a shrug. Jr was kicking up a storm, and it was so uncomfortable.

"Baby, you alright?" Ahkeem asked me. Ahkeem saw everything.

"I'm good baby. Call your brother and tell him don't be going overboard with Mya. She already has enough stuff as it is." I told him, and he nodded. Too late his ass was walking out the door with a arm full of stuff.

"Uncle Hakeem!" she screamed as she ran over to Hakeem full speed.

"Happy Birthday baby girl. You know Uncle Hakeem had to hook you up." She told her putting the bags down and picking her up.

"Sup sister in law." He spoke, reaching down hugging me. Mya didn't like that. She was one of the jealousies little girl that I knew.

"Hey baby!" he kissed Shay, and I threw up in my mouth. I just playing, I thought they were a cute couple. "Come on let's go bounce in the bouncy house. I bet I'll bet you over there." He told Mya putting her down. Mya took off full speed, my little track star.

"How are y'all doing?" I asked Shay.

"We are doing good. I never knew that I would have fell for him like I did, but I'm glad I did. You know how I felt about it in the beginning, but Hakeem changed that. Never in life would I have thought I would be this happy. I have Hakeem to think for that. I can tell you one thing Jr loves his father, and they are just alike. From the way they sleep to the way they walk." She told me laughing.

"Ouch shit." I winced in pain. "Not now Jr, today is your sister's birthday. You still have two more months to cook." I rubbed my stomach as another sharp pain ripped through my body.

"Ahkeem, she over her having contraction and telling him to wait," Shay screamed, and I could've popped her in the mouth.

"You good baby!" Ahkeem ran to my rescue.
"No, I think he's coming. Oh, God!" I screamed as I tried to

get up from the chair. Another contraction hit and I sat my ass back down.

"Come on; we need to get you to the hospital. Shay will y'all watch Mya for us, while I get her to the hospital." He asked, and she nodded.

Ahkeem helped me out the chair and Mya ran over to him and grabbed his leg. She was screaming and carrying on; you would've thought that we were leaving her ass for a week or something. "Mya daddy gotta get mommy to the hospital, I promise that I will be back." He told her, and I felt a gush of fluid running down my legs. Ready or not, this little boy was coming and fast.

When we made it my pain was at a ten. I thought they would at least stop the contraction, but because my water had broken, they were able too. Everything was going so fast! Because I was so far dilated, I couldn't get the epidural like I expected. I was mad as hell because I could feel every little thing. I can't believe that our son was finna come on Mya's birthday.
"Alright Mrs. Kadeem, let's check and see if your son is ready to enter this world." My doctor told me, and I cocked my legs wide open. I didn't care who was looking; I just wanted this baby out.

"Damn, I can see his head," Ahkeem informed us.

"Alright let's get him out. He's right there at the opening. A couple pushes, and he should be here. On three I want you to give me a push Kadeem." The doctor told me.

"You got this baby. I'ma be right here. Gimme my son." Ahkeem told me right before I started pushing.

"One, two, three, four, five, six, seven, eight, nine, ten. Relax Kadeem, get ready to give me one more push, and your son will be here." He told me, and I was exhausted.

"Ok, let's go, push!" he told me, and I gave it all I had.

"You did it, baby. Thank you for giving me, my son." Ahkeem told me, but I panic because I didn't hear him crying.

"What's wrong with my baby? Why isn't he crying?" I asked no one in particular.

"He needs a little help breathing on his own. Congratulations guys, we need to get him to the Neonatal." He told us rushing out. This was all too much for me; I broke down and cried myself to sleep.

Ahkeem

Seeing my son for the first time and him being that little had me in my feeling. I couldn't take it if something happened to him. I had to keep the faith and keep it together for Kadeem. She had done cried herself to sleep, and I snuck out to call Hakeem and check on Mya.

"Yo bruh, sis good," he asked me. That was something about my brother that I loved; he made sure that everyone was straight before anything.

"Man it's not looking too good for Jr, say a prayer for him. Kadeem cried herself to sleep, but how Mya doing." I asked.

"Man she straight, her and Jr in there watching a movie. Then two together are hell. I'll be prayer for nephew. Give Kadeem our love." He told me, and I appreciated him.

"I will bruh. Let me go down here and check on my son. I'll keep you posted." I told him ending the call.

"Excuse me, can you tell me how my son is doing? Kadeem Fisher." I told her, and she started typing in her computer.

"Y'all have a little fighter. He is on the NICU if you wanna see him, he's only 3 pounds 4 oz. We have him on machine helping him breathe and we have feeding tubes in his nose. Don't be alarmed when you see him; I can assure you that he's in good hands." She told me, and I nodded.

"Let me go let my wife know that I'm headed down to see him. Give me a minute. I don't want her to wake up, and I'm not there. We going through enough now as it is." I told her, and she nodded.

I walked back in the room, and Kadeem was sitting up on the bed staring off in space. I walked over to her and kissed her and assured her that everything was gonna be ok. I held her and let her get it all out. This was rough for me as well, but one of us needed to be strong. Both of us couldn't be a mess. Releasing her from my embrace, I dried her eyes and took a deep breath.

"I'ma go check on Jr, this might be too much for you though baby," I told her, and she nodded.

"yea, I don't think I can see him like that. Take some pictures of him though. I love you, baby." She told me, and I kissed her deeply.

When I made it to the NICU, I said a prayer before walking behind the woman. Looking at my son, I wanted to break down. He probably was small enough to fit in the palm of my hand. I just hoped that he fought enough to make it through this. My world would be turned upside down if something happened to him. I took out my phone and snapped a couple of picture, which I was unsure if I was gonna show Kadeem. She didn't need no stress on her; she just needed to worry about getting better. I couldn't take it any longer; I let the tears fall. When I got myself together, I made it back to the room that Kadeem was in. She looked like she felt a little better, so I wasn't gonna ruin that for her.

"So baby how did he look?" She asked me.

"He looks good baby; he's a fighter. Don't worry about that though, how you feeling?" I asked her changing the subject.

We sat up and talked until Kadeem went to sleep. Once she was good and knocked out, I headed to the house to check on Mya. He little ass must've had a blast at her party because she was out. She looked like she was sleeping so peaceful. I walked over to the bed and kissed her on the forehead. I grabbed my brother and hugged him.

"Thanks for looking out for Mya while we are at the hospital. Jr not looking too good man." I told him as the tears fell.

"Hell naw nigga. Like you told me earlier, Jr is a fighter. Put it God hands and watch he make it out of there." He told me, and I nodded.
"Let me get back up here before she wakes up. Tell Shay I said thank you." I told him walking out the house.

Couple months later

Jr as at his birth weight and he was being released today. There were many sleepless night, but I wouldn't change any of that. Kadeem held it together better than I thought she would when they released her. I mean she shed a couple of tears, but she had faith.

"Alright little man, come on let's get you home. I know your sister is dying to see you." I cooed to my son. He looked ever spit of Kadeem, but I was cool with that. Mya looked like me, and Jr looked like her.

"Baby hold his head right before you break his little neck." Kadeem fussed.

"Tell mam; daddy got it." I cooed at my son as I was putting him in car seat.

"Come on; let's get out of here before they find some way to keep him here." We laughed together. One of the nurses told us that Jr was a good baby and she would die to have a child like him. That shit actually scared me because I wouldn't know what to do without my little nigga.

Grabbing Kadeem's hand, we walked out the hospital like one happy family. Opening the passenger side door, I waited for Kadeem to get in and closed the door. When I buckled Jr in, I jogged around to the driver side and hopped in. Starting the car, I pulled away from the hospital. On the drive home, I thought about life and where I started from. I started off chasing Kadeem, and now we are married with two kids, and I wouldn't change it for nothing in the world. Who knew that lust would turn into love. If you would have told me five years ago that I would be married with kids, I would've laughed in your face. Love comes in all different shapes and forms, and I'm so glad that Kadeem let me in her little world.

Tyrese

Things wasn't looking too good for me. I didn't have Kadeem by my side anymore and that shit was killing me.

They say that a things that are done in the dark come to the light. I just never thought that this shit would've happened like this. I couldn't been more happy though, Angelica and I was doing better. She couldn't get enough of me, she was pregnant with another one of my babies. We decided not to find out what this one was until it was time to spit it out. Tyrese Jr was the spiting image of me and I woud forever be grateful for Angelica for giving me my son. I guess that was the good part about my life, I had family that I woudn't trade them for nothing in the world. I just wished I would've handled shit better with Kadeem though. I should have been straight up with her from the beginning and things woud've have ended the way that they did. Oh and that fuck nigga of her, I hope his ass rot in hell. He been doing the shit that I was supposed to be doing for my wife, well ex wife. A nigga will stil have love for Kadeem, no matter where we are in life.

"Baby what you over here thinking about?" Angelica asked walking over to me rubbing her belly. All these kids were doing a number on her body. She was even sexier to me with her tiger marks on her stomach. If it was up to me, I would keep her ass barefooted and pregnant. I knew that it took money to raise a family, so I needed to get on my shit.

"Life baby. I'm lucky to have a down ass chick like you. You have stuck by a nigga side through it all, and I'll forever be graceful,"

"Wouldn't have it no other way. I'm glad that you came to your senses though and got with the program. I don't know if I would be abe to live without you. Your kids and I need you," She mentioned, kissing me on the lips.

"How about we watch movies tonight and order pizza? I mentioned to her, and she nodded.

"Angel would love that. Jr will probaby fall asleep before the movie comes on. You know he can't hang," we laughed together. "Let's talk about what we gonna do about money though. You know that we don't have any income coming in because your company burned down. I mean if we need to go back to New York, lets do that. At least the house there is paid for. Once I have the baby, I can get up and find a job," she revealed shocking the hell out of me. I didn't know Angelica had it in her.

"Yea let's do that. Do you have any money left from the money that I set you monthly? Once you have the baby, we can move back there. I'll try to find something to make ends meet too. As long as our kids are good then we straight. I appreciate you for saying that you will look for a job. This made my day. Right now we gonna worry about you completing our little family. Where Angel and Jr at anyways?"

"I have a litte stash, but it ain't gonna last forever. We need a back up plan, just in case," she mentioned, and I nodded.

"Right here daddy," Angel popped up scarying the hell out of me. This little girl was my world and I knew that I had to be a better role model for her and her brother. Jr came wobbing in right behind her. My little nigga.

"We watching movies today and eating pizza. Grab the remote and find us a movie to watch. I don't wanna see Frozen, we have seen that too many time." I mentioned to her, and she nodded.

Angel was gonna be a great big sister, I could already see that She already helped out so much.When I was gone to handle business, Angel was right there caring for her mother. This baby has taking a lot out of Angelica and I couldn't wait until she gave birth. This was indeed the longest pregnancies I have seen. No matter what life throws your way, make sure you are keeping it 100 with your partner.If I woud have done that, I wouldn't be where I am today. Not that I'm not happy, I just wished I would have handled thing differently. Until next time, y'all be easy!

The

End…

Note from Author.

I enjoyed writing this book, just like I enjoyed the rest. I hate to see these characters leave. I want to thank you all for the love and support. You don't understand what this mean to me. When I first started writing, it was for fun and just for me. I first would like to thank God for giving me the gift of writing dope books. I want to thank my husband for supporting me no matter what I want to do. Next, my publisher Tyanna, thank you for giving me a chance and showing me the ropes. Thank you for being patient with me.

Last but not least, I want my lovely readers for reading and reviewing my work. I would be forever thankful for you guys. Thanks again and if you read and enjoyed, please leave me a review. Good or bad, I appreciate it all. This is not the end for me; it's only the beginning. Look out for more from me; I promise you it will be worth the wait.

CPSIA information can be obtained
at www.ICGtesting.com
Printed in the USA
LVHW112102180719
624590LV00001B/101/P

9 781095 036648